Brief

A NOVEL BY

Alexandra CHASIN

Brief

a novel by

Alexandra Chasin

Jaded Ibis Press
sustainable literature by digital means.™
an imprint of Jaded Ibis Productions U.S.A.

ISBN: 978-1-937543-24-2

Library of Congress Control Number: 2012920914

Published by Jaded Ibis Press, sustainable literature by digital means™ An imprint of Jaded Ibis Productions, LLC USA
http://jadedibisproductions.com

This book is also available as an interactive app, ebook, and fine art limited editions. Visit our website for more information.
jadedibisproductions.com

Cover design and art by Hugh Sansom.

For Richard and Laura Chasin, who rock

A Note from the Publisher

You hold in your hands a paperback edition of Alexandra Chasin's novel, *Brief.* Although we're confident you'll enjoy this remarkably intelligent and witty story about an art vandal charged with defacing a masterpiece of modern art, we want you to know that this paperback is not *the whole story*, so to speak.

Jaded Ibis Press first published *Brief* as an interactive app for the iPad, the device for which it was specifically written. Chasin designed the narrative to incorporate the medium as an integral part of the message: Maybe the way we turn out is less the fault of our parents and more the effect of larger cultural and historical influences — maybe history is the real culprit.

The digital application, developed by Scott Peterman, randomly locates color and grayscale images from a cache of over 600, then wraps the story's text around them. The images are not intended to illustrate the text but rather to evoke the novel's time period and storyline, probing the role of cause and effect in history. Swiping or tapping the screen forward or backward changes the images, so that the chances of any one screen repeating itself are nearly 4,000,000 to one. Images can also be changed by gently shaking the tablet.

Because the screens of *Brief* are non-repeating, each reader reaches a significantly different experience and shifting meanings. This paper book, therefore, is like a snapshot of the app — the equivalent of one meaning out of the millions of possibilities available within the app edition.

We hope that you, as an attentive reader, consider your own role in the randomness of history: how the decisions you make (paper or app?) — combined with decisions others make for us and those randomly tumbling out of history's cache — may influence the outcome of you and your life.

Enjoy!

Since the object in question is a modern poem,
A police spokesman stated yesterday,
It is hard to tell whether it has been damaged
Or not or how badly.
—D. J. Enright

I have requested an oral argument

because I'd like to try, if I may, to explain why my representation and I have chosen this defense, uncommon though it is, and why I would take issue with the psychiatrists' findings. Of *course* they came up with *bupkus*. I say this with all due respect. After all, Your Honor, Mother and Dad are blameless, as blameless as anyone who has caused a birth could be, given that no child ever asks to be born (as most will find some occasion later on for throwing back in their parents' faces). If there's not a bad egg on the face of the family portrait, the orthodoxtors can't add it up — but they're missing the big picture. Can I just say something about that, briefly?

My parents got along just fine. They rarely quarreled, except perhaps about whether to bring deviled eggs or potato salad to the 4th of July picnic at the Hatfields', or which route to take to the Capulets' Kwanzaa (né Christmas)

party. Mild-mannered, Mother and Dad planted in spring and tended garden in summer, harvesting and canning fruit in fall, and eating last summer's tomatoes next winter. They chuckled and they tsked. They helped me with my homework, until they no longer could. They went abroad only once, and then to Canada, but neither one ever ran for president, so it can't be held against them. If Mother hooked a few too many rugs, what matter? And if Dad collected miniature doohickeys, what harm? They always provided, and sometimes they took me to church. They watched TV.

Then what explains me? The head shrinkers met to disagree and made no headway. They quavered and quacked out in the hall; they did the *yes yes sure sure* when they came into the room. They even did a few more tests. The first page of the chart showed my name, date of birth, last address, sex, race, social, and insurance information (but is anybody really covered for this kind of thing?). On the second page, the broken lines called for my military service, felonies, surgeries, previous psychiatric treatment — all

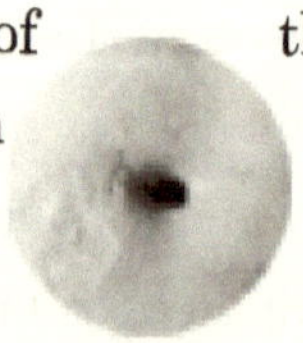

blank, except my educational background, which overflowed the space allotted. My overeducation in the irony tower in fits and starts. The third page remained empty, awaiting the narrative, the family history, but there was no accord on how to enter the absence of data. One case of asthma on the part of the paternal great-grandfather, a recurring carbuncle on the foot of an aunt, but none of the pokes, prods, or popsicle sticks has produced anything psychological.

Within the domestic sphere, the doctors could find no history to speak of. Mother like her mother, Dad like his dad. No trauma, no abuse of substance, child, or spouse, no neglect going back and back. Just: Homestead. High school. Honest trading at the town crossroads. A couple of mentions in the newspaper: strictly local heroics involving pets. In the whole family tree, no one out of his or hers. 'Til me. 'Til that fateful day. The authorities flipped back to the first page, and reviewed my date of birth. *Hmmm, January 30, 1961, very interesting*, they said, as they stroked each other's beards. *Old enough to know better,* they concluded, *sane and able to stand trial,* but they totally missed the point.

The point is, Your Honor, shit happened — shit did happen — but not in the course of my toilet training, if you get my meaning. The relevant history begins back before I was born, before I was even a twinkle in the eye, and before the eyes that beheld me first were themselves twinkles. It begins a few millennia ago when Moses came upon the idolators dancing, and saw the famous golden calf. He got hot under the tunic. He pulled down the idols, he brake them, brake them, brake them. He cast down the calf, burnt it in the fire, ground it into powder, strewed it with water, and made the chili. Yes, Your Honor, I'll try to be serious. The Qu'ran would concur: it is Major Shirk to revere material objects, to make them in the image of, or associate them with, divinity. So I've got something in common with Moses and Major Shirk: we believe in the astonishing world-changing power of representation. Excuse me? Yes, I will establish the relevance, of course. This is crucial background. Headlines referred to me as the "High Art Killer" and "Cuckoo Connoisseur," but the vandal took the handle. I mean, my nom-de-plume-de-guerre is Inqui. Check it on the chart, "Inqui," with the quotation marks, as though they don't believe me.

Or maybe the story begins on May 21, 1972, when Lazlo Toth smashed one of the mightiest symbols of art anywhere, the *Pietà*, Shirk of Shirks, with a sledgehammer, shouting, "I am Jesus Christ risen from the dead." It was his 33rd birthday, the day he popped the virgin's elbow, a chunk of her nose, and a chip of her eyelid. She wept, but she'd been weeping all along. Him, he was nuts — Toth, I mean — totally doubledecker, got two years in a booth like the rubber-walled one where I've been hanging my hat, but in Australia. No accident he was a geologist, used to breaking rocks with a hammer, good at it. He made quite an impression — on the sculpture and on the radicals who took up the call, "No more

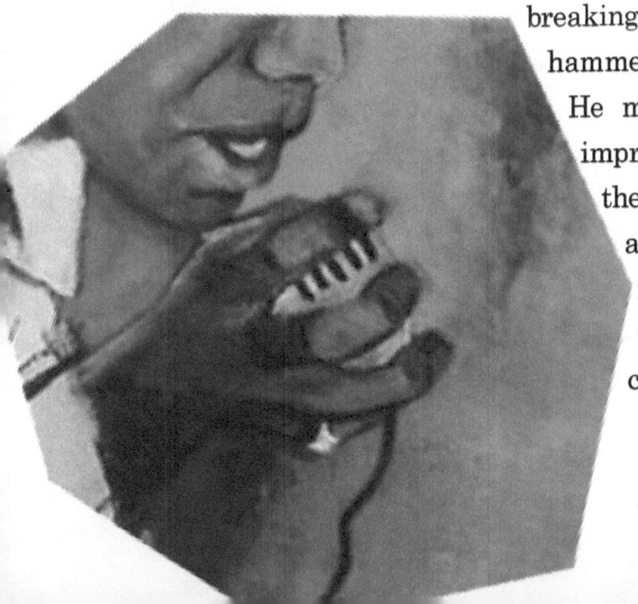

masterpieces!" On me. I was 11 at the time. First time I ever had an inkling of how I might answer the question, what did I want to be when I grew up? Emphasis on *when, when* did I grow up — *when* did I *do* anything at all?

The answer to any question of any human origin and its antecedent always lies further back than you think, somewhere between...prehistory and now. The answer is always an ambigram — oh, I'm sorry, that's a typographical form that can be read from more

than one direction or orientation. The relevance? I already tried to explain this to the shrinks. I'm talking about when I was born, Your Honor, *1961*. Same upside-down as right-side up. January 30, to be specific. That week, The Innocents' "Gee Whiz" debuted on the pop charts, which was — you could argue, and people would soon enough — art itself. The mouths of even the oldest doctors hung open as they tried to name that tune, and to picture my folks wheezing at the casserole-bearing neighbors' negligible humor, as the latter — one bearing the casserole and the other bearing their own newborn baby — pointed to me

and my wrinkles, trilling the title, and *Looky there, so adorable, the original Innocent.* There they are down the wrong end of the telescope, my folks and the neighbors, propping me and my crinkly

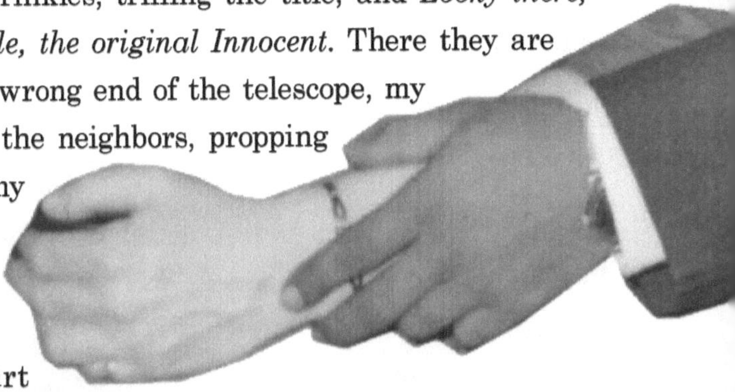

counterpart up with cushions on the sofa to watch *American Bandstand* with them, and parrying with another chart-topper of the moment, "Baby Sittin' Boogie." Maybe Dick Clark is my real father.

Count backwards with me, if you will, month month month, back to April 1960. Now maybe we're getting somewhere. It is entirely possible that I was conceived the day that a "weather plane" crashed in the Soviet Union, its pilot having had "difficulties with his oxygen equipment." Or so went Washington's official statement regarding the capture of CIA operative Gary Powers and his Lockheed U-2 in Sverdlovsk. Having penetrated enemy territory at the moment that Soviet technology was finally capable of detecting foreign bodies over home skies, Powers was shot down. He parachuted into the hands of the KGB. His equipment apparently in better working order, my father and his little U-2 fell into friendlier hands, his mission arguably more successful, arguably less — I've done some damage, but I have not yet derailed *détente* or thrown a wrench in global political proceedings.

Throwing hammers, now that's another story. Some of my colleagues have gotten into that act, like the guys who threw one at a portrait of Jesse Jackson called *How Ya Like Me Now*? when it was being installed in Washington, some years back. In the painting, Jesse was made out like the original white devil, blue eyes, blond hair, the whole nine yards, or rather 14 by 16 feet. Brothers thought the painting was racist, even if the artist was Black. Come to find out that Jesse not only got "a kick" out of the painting, he had a solid aesthetic theory too: "Sometimes art provokes; sometimes it angers. That is a measure of its success. Sometimes it inspires creativity. Maybe the sledgehammers should have been on display too." Like he was channeling Marcel.

Marcel Duchamp, that is, whose objective with his Readymades was "to go into the infra-thin interval that separated two identical things." Like Jesse and Jesse? When Robert Rauschenberg asked Duchamp, in the year of my birth, "So you want to destroy art for all mankind?" Duchamp answered, "No, only for myself." Check brother Marcel again: "I despise *Guernica* in its glass nightwatch...I hate the glass that prevents my knife from opening vaginas in the damned canvas...I hate the Gioconda moustache

of *Guernica*...." How ya like him now? And they think *Shafrazi* did shit to *Guernica*.

Back to Jesse's point though, some people might find that the CIA and the KGB provoke and anger, and/or inspire creativity. Maybe their success depends where you're standing, or flying, which frontlines you fall behind. Who, or what, is hanging, being hanged? Where, when, and how. Upside-down or right-side up? Right-to-left or left-to-right? Mother up and Dad down or vice versa, from Eisenhower to Carter to Reagan and back. Maybe Winifred was also conceived the day Powers hit

the ground running. What's the difference? Winnie and I were identicals in so many ways, separated at first by little more than the B & M from Boston, and later we turned out to be the two possibilities — but I'm getting ahead of myself. Stay tuned.

Mother and Dad and I met our neighbors Frank and Irene the day Winnie and I were born. Irene lay recuperating in the room next to my mother's in the Boston Lying-In Hospital, having given birth to Winifred Rebelda nine hours and 45 minutes after my mother gave birth to me. Three days later, Mother and Irene were calling to each other through the wall, exchanging cremes and magazines. Winnie and I waited and watched, twinned in two ways, and by such small accident. Turned out Frank and Irene, and now Winnie, lived just a few blocks from us in the same suburb on the North Shore, on opposite sides of the literal track, but the same side of the redlines on the bankers' maps, where they, Frank and Irene, spent prime time dreaming of a

little restaurant business, rush-hour traffic in prime rib. Just because we happened to be fresh-squeezed,

Winnie and I, at the same place and time, our peer group would be defined each by the other. It's like Rauschenberg said that same year. He knew that his *White Paintings* would yellow, and would need to be repainted, perhaps at such a time as he could no longer do it himself: "It is completely irrelevant that I am making them — today is their creator." That is the shit. If I may.

From a more pedestrian, if not proletarian, perspective: it all began on the factory floor, sometime between the origins of Judeo-Islamo-Christian culture and late spring 1960, when a particular haploid chromosome packed into a certain spermatozoon delivered the DNA corsage to the cytoplasm of the oocyte that answered the door. My maternal and paternal pronuclei pulled themselves together, and that night they danced with the jerky new movements of youth in those years. It is no longer thought that they merged completely, but rather that their membranes dissolved, allowing the two chromosomes to align on the spindle apparatus at the equator. Zygote, embryo, embryo, embryo, embryo, morula, which is to say, in Latin, I looked like a mulberry. There followed the hatching of the blastocyst — *pop!* — which is typical. Within twenty-one days, my ectoblast cells migrated through the primitive streak and formed the mesoblast. Thanks to the proliferation and migration of epiblast cells in the direction of my embryonic disk's median line, my cranial region was strengthened by the epiblast cells and so formed the primitive pit with the primitive node.

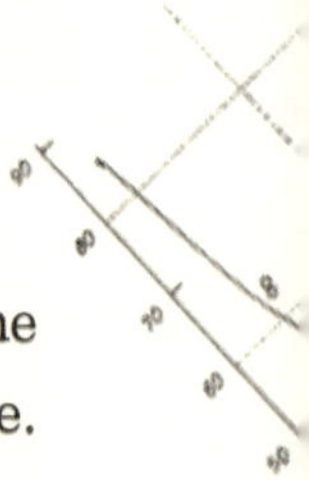

Does that explain the *pop, pop, pop* that was the hatching of bullets as the South African police opened fire on unarmed Black protesters in the Sharpeville Massacre the same week? You be the judge. Heh heh. Near Sharpeville, but 3,000 years earlier, in the primitive pits of Ukhahlamba-Brakensberg, San shamans applied minerals to the cave walls with finger, flint, and bone. In Somaliland, artists painted themselves or real or imagined others worshipping red and purple humpless cows. And why not? My god, why not? I've seen the mammoth and the auroch on the walls and ceilings painted 22,000 years ago by artists in Southern France, drawings high and low, and I touched some of the human genitalia represented there when the docent wasn't looking. I've been a believer ever since. Still extant: handprints in the caves at Maros

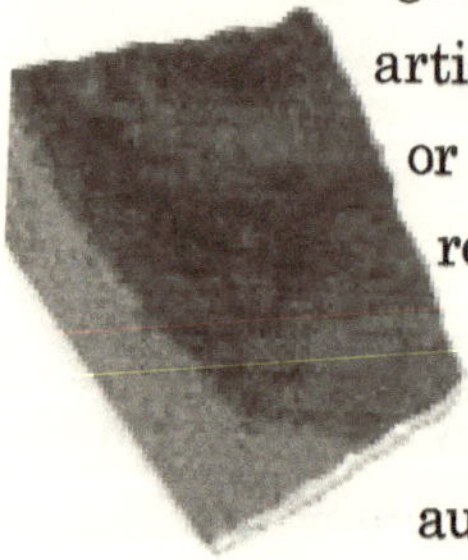

in Sulawesi, ochre in Australia, and paintings from Wadi Kubbaniya to Blackwater Draw. Maybe as long as 100,000 years ago, people drew. They drew. We drew and still we draw. To draw power from the walls, to bless the hunt, to court, to count, to make things beautiful or true to life? The same "we" do not know; it's dark in them thar caves.

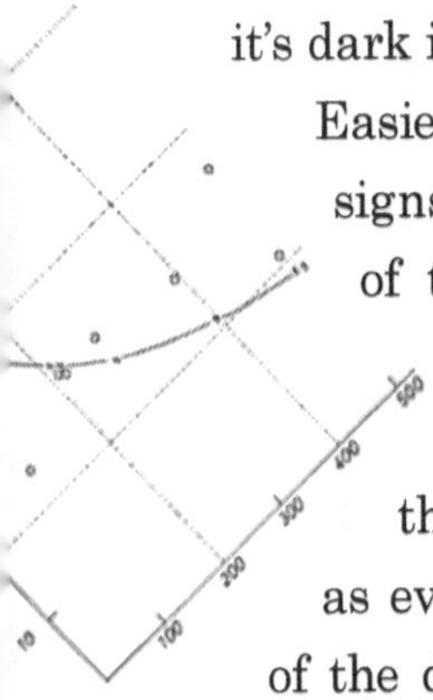

Easier to shine a light into, or rather, listen for signs of life at the door of, the cave of the mother of the modern *Homo sapiens sapiens*. By the tenth week, my brain was producing almost 250,000 new neurons every minute, and the week after that, my sex would have been as evident as it would ever be. The nightly news of the day coursed through the amniotic fluid that surrounded me. Powers was charged with espionage. I got organs. He was sentenced to 10 years in prison. I got arms and legs. Unbeknownst to me, Winnie was similarly extruding limbs in another ranch on a neighboring street, let's call it "around the corner." Let's call her "the girl next door." Unthinkable to me now: a time when I not only did not know her, I didn't even have a twinge of an intuition that she was somewhere out there, or in there, developing on a parallel course. *But still unstoried, artless, unenhanced, Such as she was, such as she would become.*

As we continued to bake in our atomic ovens, Chad, Benin, Nigeria, Ivory Coast, Madagascar, Central African Republic, Mali, Niger, Senegal, Burkina Faso, Mauritania, Togo, Zaire, Somalia, Congo, Gabon, and Cameroon gained independence. Millions of people became citizens of sovereign states that had formerly, and for so long, been colonies from which metropoles had sucked human resources — slaves — as well as natural resources from straw to gold. One by one, the countries of Africa claimed names in local languages and said in those languages, *Ready or not, here we govern ourselves.* What is the sound of one fetus clapping?

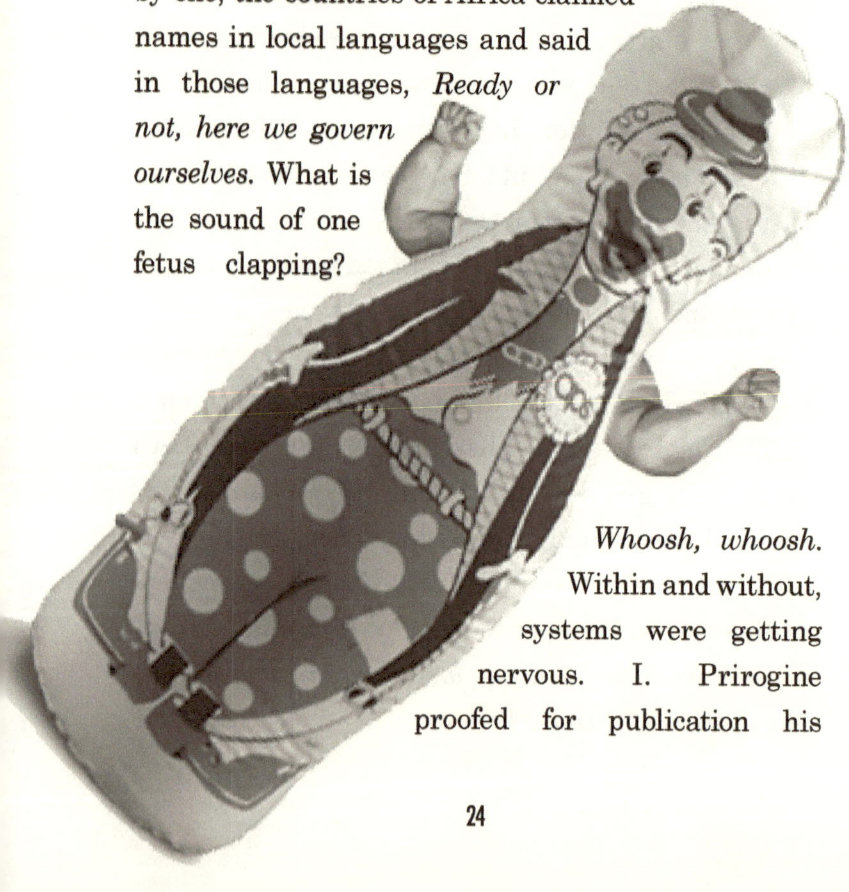

Whoosh, whoosh. Within and without, systems were getting nervous. I. Prirogine proofed for publication his

thermodynamic proof of a nonlinear dissipative system far from equilibrium that evolves irreversibly.

I've heard it said that the human ear is homologous with the whole human embryo, which I think, frankly, must be horseshit. But there is plenty of evidence that the intrauterine environment of the homunculus does affect personality development, and even vacuum-packed within it, the coiled-up being attracts information. The doctors — real ones, not those Marx and Freud Brothers — seem to think so. On the other hand, they also say the child responds more to what is unheard than what is heard, what is unsaid more than what is said; this is the meaning of ultrasound. Thus the zeitgeist will out — and/or in — and the uncanny, the ESP, if you will, of the human child, is to receive, to collect its message through the amniotic medium — if he or she can just make it out — and to transduce. Maybe Mother and Dad should have played Mozart for me, but they were no Einsteins. Anyway, this was before store shelves were swollen with items aimed at making genius babies out of pink and red tissue.

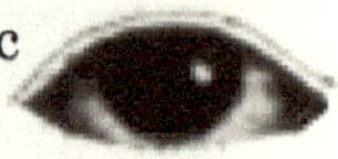

In my mother's last month of pregnancy — "I-minus-one" I call it — John F. Kennedy was sworn in as President of the United States, on a snowday that shut down the East Coast. As the sage and grizzled poet, Robert Frost, stood to ennoble the inauguration with a recitation, he was blinded by the sun. Therefore, he literally couldn't read "The Dedication" he had written for the occasion, and had to substitute "The Gift Outright." Because he knew this one by heart:

> The land was ours before we were the land's.

What do you mean, "ours," grizzly man? But I digress.

> She was our land more than a hundred years
> Before we were her people. She was ours
> In Massachusetts, in Virginia,

But we were England's, still colonials,
Possessing what we still were unpossessed by,
Possessed by what we now no more possessed.
. . .
Such as we were we gave ourselves outright
(The deed of gift was many deeds of war)
To the land vaguely; realizing westward,
But still unstoried, artless, unenhanced,
Such as she was, such as she would become.

Analyze that, motherfuckers. Excuse me, I meant to say, "Exhibit A."

To "The Gift," I could *relate.* As I set about to dissolve the bands that withheld me from the land of living, I knew myself to be still unstoried and artless. I had heard much, but I had seen nothing, and like Jack Frost, stood, at that moment, to be blinded by the literal light, to become such as I would become, and now am. But *this* — "The Dedication" that went unsaid, and snatches of which spiraled in through my umbilicus, hereinafter called "Exhibit B" — this I could *grok*:

Summoning artists to participate
In the august occasions of the state
Seems something artists ought to celebrate.
Today is for my cause a day of days.

there ar

It was not our day yet, but this prospect had me turning in the belly of the beast...

Goes back to the beginning of the end
Of what for centuries had been the trend;
A turning point in modern history.

. . . kicking at the sac wall. It was a call to battle . . . not just bad poetry, but something bigger.

Some poor fool has been saying in his heart
Glory is out of date in life and art.
Our venture in revolution and outlawry
Has justified itself in freedom's story
Right down to now in glory upon glory.

Crumpled up in the contorted syntax that follows, an unfortunately incisive reference to hard currency, and to us, its distribution network in pink and blue, the 200 million tributaries of the flow of paper capital, each with a referent, a one-to-one correspondence with a unit of gold in Fort Knox, as a certificate could be ordered to attest:

emc
babes

Now came on a new order of the ages
That in the Latin of our founding sages
(Is it not written on the dollar bill

We carry in our purse and pocket still?)
God nodded his approval of as good.

E pluribus unum. Meaning: out of many, one. Out of many messages, one baby. At a time. The baptism and the benediction. Out of many dollars, the one from out of which God Washington glares with the one eye atop the pyramid. The birth of credit, meaning unmoored to bullion.

Current events corroborated. Nearer my God, the farthing coin went off the market in the U.K. and farther away, at the start of the same new year, German atonalist Winifried Zillig's "The Sacrifice" was revived in West Germany. It sounded like shit, but "It's pure opera," said the composer as the chorus of penguins on a glacier intoned their farewell to the explorer Robert Scott disappearing into the Antarctic night. In utero, it sounded more like *whoosh* *whoosh*, but what didn't? Ultrasonographers on all sides of the Iron Curtain rushed to hear said *whoosh* in their Cold-War way, the race for outer space matched by a race for inner space. No, my mother was not the first pregnant woman to go under the transducer, but she was close

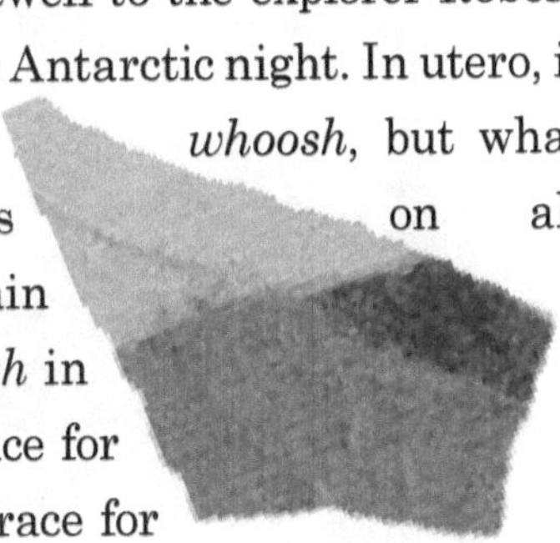

in time, if not in space. Just west of the Curtain, and north of the penguins, in Sachsenwald, former SS Sturmbannführer Richard Baer, the last unaccounted-for commandant of Auschwitz, was caught bending over a power saw impersonating a lumberjack in a dark forest on a foggy morning. Maybe Robert Scott was my granddad, or maybe the ersatz lumberjack grandspawned Winnie. She and I were almost born.

On January 4, 1961, General Maxwell D. Taylor replaced John D. Rockefeller the 3rd as the second President of Lincoln Center for the Performing Arts, Inc. It didn't seem right, a soldier running that show, but I was in no position, no shape, at that time, to be

making a statement to the press. The doctor said I was engaged, not *on-gah-ZHAY,* with a foot still tucked under my mother's rib, and my whole body still coiled like a conch held up to my own ear, chasing my own vestigial tail, never making any progress, *whoosh whoosh* the main medium of my days. Taylor would be recalled to active military duty on July 1, 1961, and would resign his post in the arts on July 10 to become the military representative to President Kennedy, a crosswiring, and an inheritance, that might explain the difference between Winnie's fate and mine. Meanwhile, back at the ranch, President Eisenhower severed diplomatic and consular relations with Cuba, and an atomic reactor exploded at the National Reactor Testing Station in Idaho Falls. "Only" three military technicians were killed. Mother and Dad made one last stab at conjugal relations — doctor's orders notwithstanding. Dad exploded in her hands but no one was hurt.

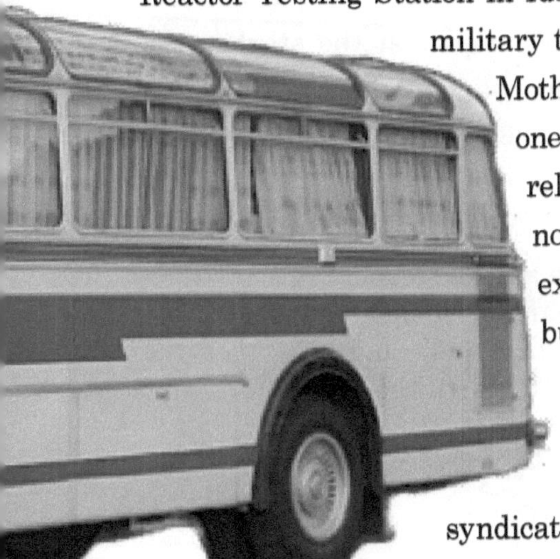

I honor as my godfather — no, I make no reference to syndicated crime, which I call

TV reruns; I speak spiritually here — the Italian sculptor Alfredo Fioravanti, who walked into the U.S. consulate in Rome in 1961 to confess that he had had a hand in forging the Etruscan terracotta warriors then on display in the Metropolitan Museum of Art. Back in the nineteen-teens, he had helped a couple of brothers make the sculptures, age them to perfection, and sell them for a pretty farthing, or lire, really, lots and lotsa lire. But Fioravanti had held on to the fragment of clay thumb that fit right onto the warrior's hand better than the second half of a Jell-O box, which was how he proved his participation in the fraud. His shenanigans, or maybe his naked shamelessness, roused me to action; like the whistle blown by the umpire at the start of the game, this story made me want to play too, dabble in the arts. Not just dabble…rouse rabble. Had I not not heard that

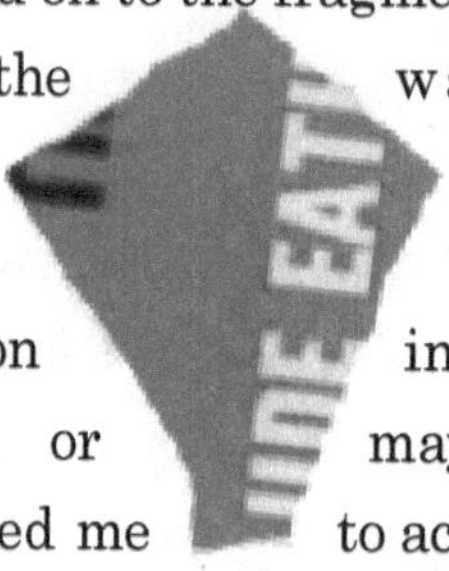

> There is a call to life a little sterner,
> And braver for the earner, learner, yearner?
> Less criticism of the field and court
> And more preoccupation with the sport?

Question marks mine.

It makes the prophet in us all presage
The glory of a next Augustan age
Of a power leading from its strength and pride
Of young ambition eager to be tried.

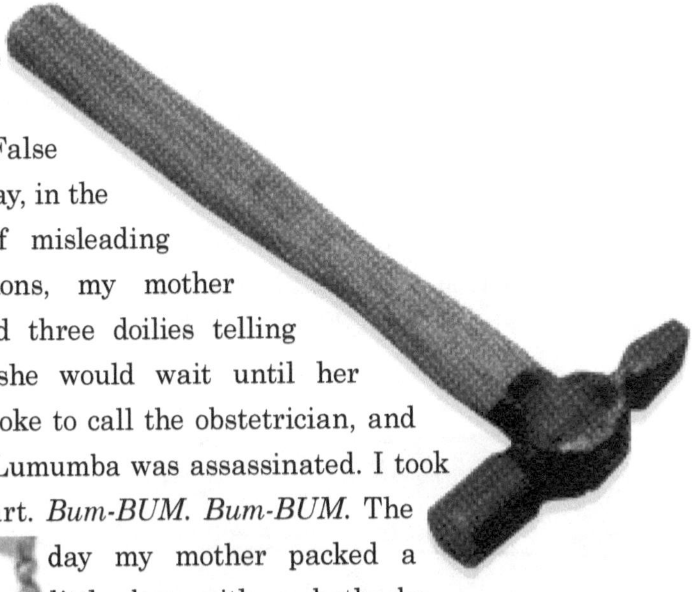

U n t i e
me now.

On False Labor Day, in the midst of misleading contractions, my mother crocheted three doilies telling herself she would wait until her water broke to call the obstetrician, and Patrice Lumumba was assassinated. I took it to heart. *Bum-BUM. Bum-BUM.* The

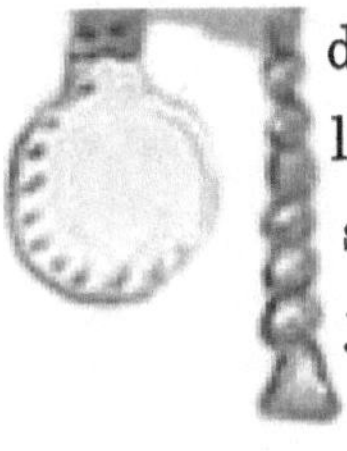

day my mother packed a little bag with a bathrobe, slippers, and knitting needles, a rightist junta ousted a junta accused of "leftist excesses" in El Salvador. On the domestic front, my nucleotides were right on course. *Mother,* I said, *whoosh whoosh. Get it? Nuclear tides.* Mother doubled over, probably not in laughter. The same day, the Soviets freed the two surviving crewmen of a U.S. reconnaissance plane they had shot down the summer before over the Barents Sea, as JFK announced in the first-ever live presidential news conference.

The same month, in France, a referendum supported Charles de Gaulle's policies in Algeria. More on that later. Nine months and nine days later, to be precise. That's how long some things take to gestate. Maybe DeGaulle was established as one of my internal organs. As Frost had not said:

> Colonial had been the thing to be
> As long as the great issue was to see
> What country'd be the one to dominate
> By character, by tongue, by native trait....

With this, the poet may have equated Us with Them, but the note of sympathy might have been less favorably received in equatorial Africa, even discounting aesthetic offenses.

> We see how seriously the races swarm
> In their attempts at sovereignty and form.
> They are our wards we think to some extent
> For the time being and with their consent,
> To teach them how Democracy is meant.

Familiar paternalism from a pater familias, galling

indeed. Authorities in London brought to light a false-bottomed cigarette lighter spies had stuffed silly with secrets about the HMS Dreadnought; said secrets had been bound for Moscow by way of high-powered wireless, until those spies went shopping. Like the tin of film in their shopping bag, Winnie and I were undeveloped but not unaffected.

In quick succession: Perry Mason solved "The Case of the Fickle Fortune," in which a newly discovered cache of greenbacks goes missing; a U.S. B-52 bomber with two 24-megaton nuclear bombs crashed near Goldsboro, North Carolina; and Bob Dylan homed in on New York City. Almost coincidentally, a B-52 crashed in New Mexico, and the Fed said the two nuclear bombs ejected prior to the crash were unarmed. Then-Defense Secretary Robert McNamara now says otherwise: we came *this close* to nuclear disaster. *Mother,* I said, *Sit tight. Mother,* I said, *'Grok' means to understand so thoroughly that the observer becomes a part of the observed—to merge, blend, intermarry, lose identity in group experience. It means almost everything that we mean by religion, philosophy, and science—and it means as little to us as color means to a blind person.* Here too, membranes dissolve. *Mother,* I said,

you'll see — or is it I who will see? We'll see.

Daily nightly news, plain dealing, *Bee Sun Digest*, trial tribulation *Tribune*, hark *Herald*. Then: the canned tomatoes fell to the floor; her water broke — there was no mistaking it. *Honey — the bag — by the door.* The pains came more often until they became veritably VHF. On the way to the hospital, the becoming itself accelerated to Ultra High Frequency. Then, suddenly, something shrill and arrhythmic, the red the white the black the blue, the beauty and the gore, the blur, the me the all the it, a slimy green-backed toad, something that would be seen. Thus, like the Stranger in the proverbial Strange Land, I came, Lord I came, into these several United States...likewise not entirely green. *E Pluribus Unum.*

Whatwith, SPLAT, I was born. I, Inqui. One Dexter Scott was born the same day to Martin Luther King, Jr., so it's unlikely the latter is my father, or things might have turned out different. If the flap of a butterfly's wing in China makes a difference, how does the contingency of paternity, or any mutation that attends it, register on the Richter scale of history, which

seems to have supplied so many fathers and mothers, forebears and forces, influences and coincidences, reasons and random long-term and proximate causes of first then and now now? Events, ideas, institutions, practices, and their prime movers, people. Righteous, fucked up, all for one and all, to a person, if there is such a thing in this unholy pigmented crisis of a world, but all signs point to...signs. Yes, I'm trying to be brief. Please bear with me.

Dexter and I were followed by one Winifred Rebelda. Because Irene had taken thalidomide during her pregnancy to counter her morning sickness — sorry, Your Honor, bad joke — she was one of the last women to do so — there was some suspense built into

5 6 9 12 BELL TELEPHONE HOUR—Music

COLOR Disneyland is the setting for "The Sounds of America." Details in the Close-up below. (60 min.)

Shooting this show in Disneyland presented problems. See pages 12 and 13.

7 S(
"Race /
a New
been p
are una
Lee Pa

Barbara
Pamela
9 7
Ty Har
mer m
deal fo
steal h
the ins
thereaf
Spence
ard Lo

Guest Cast

Drew Dekker .... Ty Hardin
Martiza Vedar ...... Kathleen Crowley
Nona Rumson .... Lee Patrick
Holtz Von Ulrich .... Oscar Bergi

9:30 2 PONY EXPRESS—Western
"Showdown at Thirty Mile Ridge." A
kill a Pony Ex-
thinks murdered
n. George Snow:
ders: Jack Elam.
ASON
HT ZONE
ipet" is rerun.
own can't get a
or hit the high
'n and steps in
:k. Joey Crown:
ing is host.
R
MICHAEL
Marty Maxwel
humor—he plans

Winnie's birth. But the latter emerged with a good APGAR score, and with ten fingers and ten toes. Winnie's psychophocomelia didn't manifest until later. That's a folk diagnosis: *psycho*, as in *psycho*, p-h-o-c-o-m-e-l-i-a. Anyway, Winnie's G for Grimace, or reflexivity, was especially strong. Meanwhile, in other post-natal rooms at the Boston Lying-In, mothers who had taken D.E.S. — do I need to spell that — Diethylstilbestrol — were participating in a study about the results of that chemical protection against miscarriage. A little Librium might depress a fetus, ironically, but reproductive systems were thrown into major disequilibrium with some of those miracles of modern medicine. The good news was that the transmission of hepatitis had cast serious doubts on the wisdom of using syringes and needles more than once. Patient safety and the inescapable dictum that "time is money" gave rise to

TV CLOSE-UP GUIDE

'TH ... ICA'

-Music

COLO
origin
Jenkir
Jacqu
actors
1
60-mi
sical
specia
of ye
Main
self c
Smith.

Highlights

"Wish upon a Star" D'Amboise, Ruth Earl
"Bessie and Tessie" ..Nelson, Earl Twins
"Mark Twain Remembers" ....Marfield
"Island, a Tree House and a Cave" ..Lane
"It's a Scandal to the Jay Birds" ..Chorus
"This Day Is Your Day"
...........Nelson, D'Amboise, Earl Twins

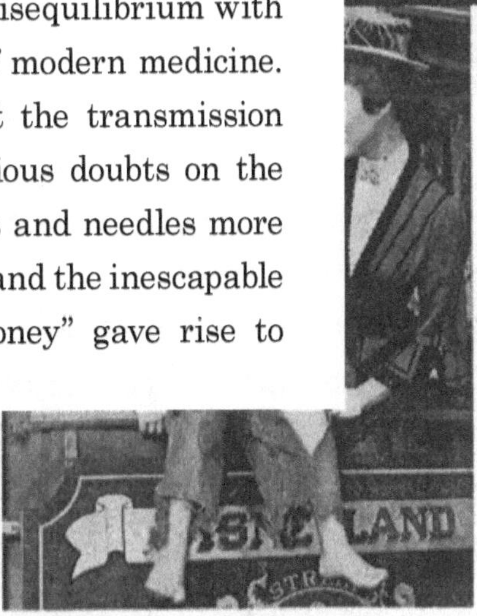

The Earl Twins and Scott Lane

a demand for disposable injection systems, so the staff at Boston Lying-In were using the new Plastipak polypropylene disposables.

Irene lay-in in the room to one side of my mother. On the other side, Wayne C. Booth gave birth to *The Rhetoric of Fiction*, in which he established distinctions between the "real" and the "implied" authors of a narrative — and between "reliable" and "unreliable" narrators. The fallibility of memory means that the writer must necessarily be an unreliable narrator. Also contributing to unreliability in a narrator, in memoir as in fiction: the fractured, compound, shifting, and recombinatory character of the self, ditto with respect to linguistic structures that call forth narrators. So whether I was authored by self or others is a question for the ages, for the sages, for who can say that context does not write this courtroom drama. See what I mean?

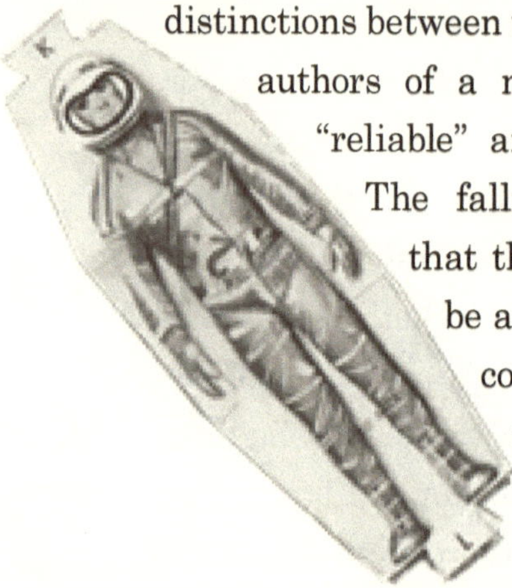

Then let me give a little more context. Back in the winter of the year of the publication of *The Winter of Our Discontent*, as I learned first to breathe air and then to suck, a

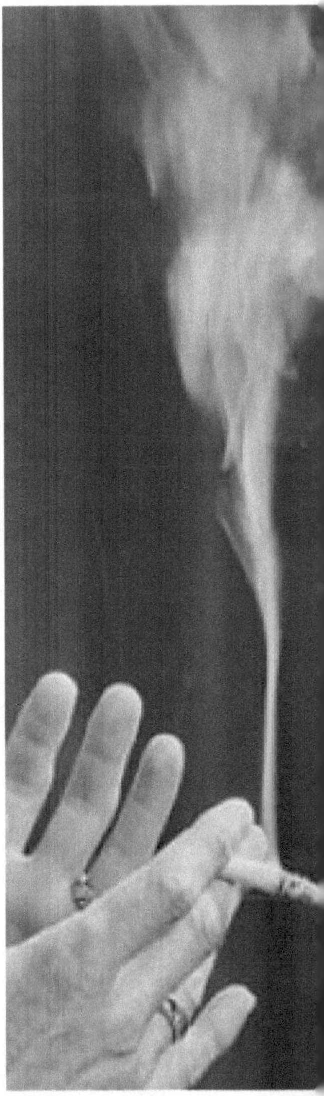

male chimpanzee named Ham, who outweighed me by 30 pounds, learned not to. Ham was rocketed into space to test the Project Mercury capsule, like the royal taster of spaceship life, the bellwether, the canary in the coalmine of the still satelliteless sky. The day I was vaccinated, Adolf Eichmann went on trial in Jerusalem for crimes against humanity. It turned out he was a regular joe, indistinguishable from the rest of us humanities. From variations on banality, as we shall see in the case of Winnie, nobody is immune, even if we don't share needles, none of us inhuman. My R for Respiration, which classified as "lusty" at birth, remained intense: I cried — in fact, I howled — but nobody banned it as obscene when I did. Anybody would have a reaction.

I smelled baby powder. The baby batting on the blanket with me was Winnie — I reached out for her with little kicks. When the corner of her mouth was touched or stroked, she turned her head and opened her mouth to "root" in the

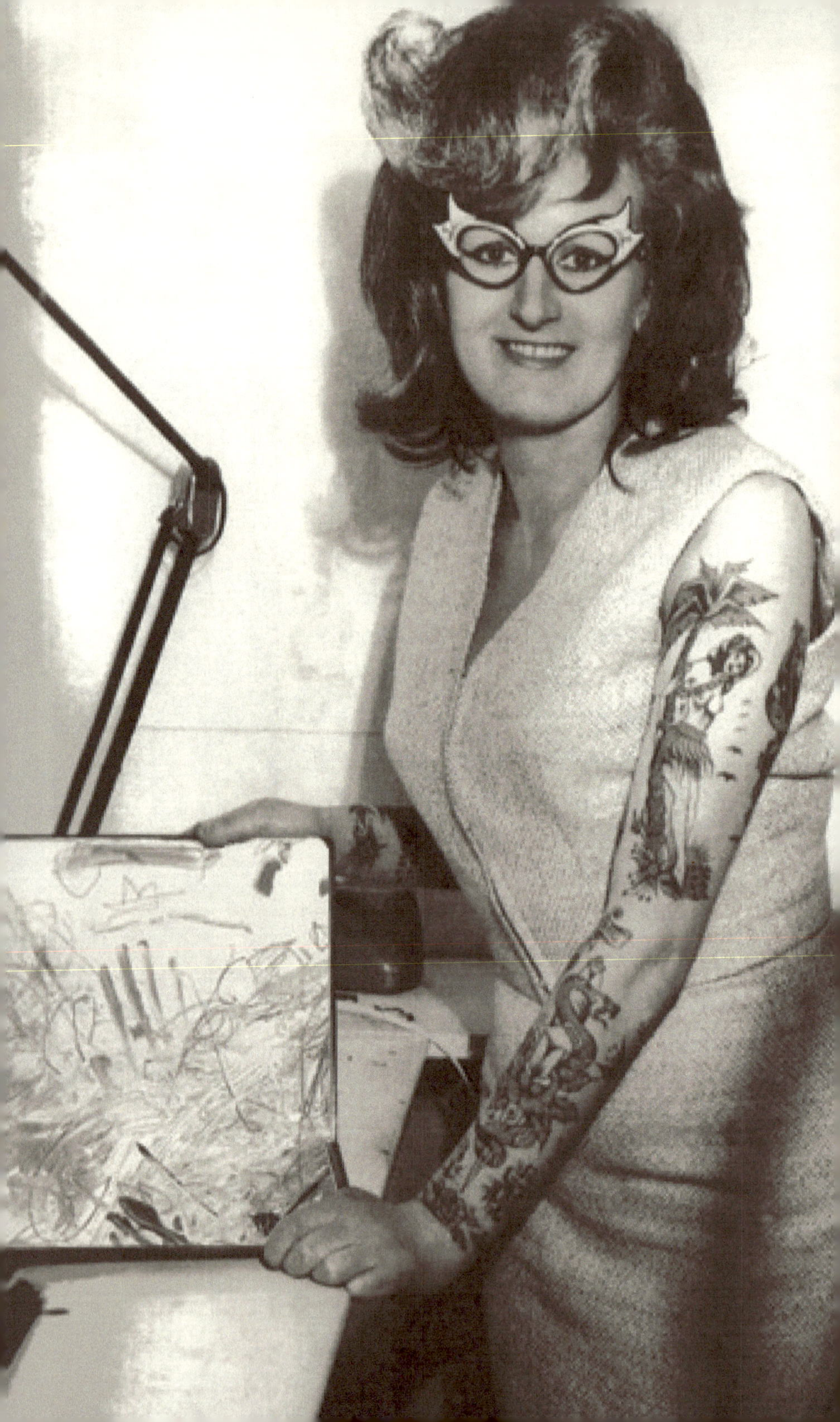

direction of the stroking. The root reflex pointed Winnie toward the Portuguese Colonial War in Angola; she chewed, in turn, on its root causes. The Moro reflex, or the so-called "startle" reflex, was triggered when I heard a sudden loud noise; I threw back my head, and threw out my arms and legs when Vostok 1 blasted off, carrying the first human being into outer space, and then again at the sound of retrofire near Angola as the Soviet rocket reentered Earth's atmosphere. Yuri Gagarin parachuted back down to its surface in the U.S.S.R. He knew exactly how lucky he was, boy. We wouldn't be so concerned with a Moro again for another seventeen years, by which time it would be clear to me that just as all Western-Art-historical roads had led from, all aphoristical roads also led back to, Rome. Oh, Rome, me, oh. But in babeland, stroking my palm triggered the grasp reflex, which lasted until the invasion of the Bay of Pigs, which was so hard to grasp, the reflex relaxed. Just what could I hold on to? Not Secretary of State Dean Rusk's announcement that "there is not and will not be any intervention there by United States forces." I thought I smelled a smoking gun — was it really an exploding cigar or was that a cartoon joke?

Although I had blurry vision, I could focus fairly well on objects at about eight to 14 inches — the distance from my mother's face to mine when she was holding me in her arms. It would take another few months to make out distinct figures on the TV, but I could hear Alan Shepard blast off in Freedom 7, trailing the Cosmonaut to become the first American in space, because this flight, unlike that of the Vostok, was televised. If my sight was still unfolding, I nevertheless had a very well-developed sense of smell that made me very choosy about my favorite scent. The development of my senses may have been normal, but my sense of developments was that they were rather alarming. In the first days of life, I could recognize my mother's natural scent and liked it best of all. Within a couple of weeks, I came to recognize the smells of Huntley, Brinkley, Cronkite, and liked them best of all. Remember when the anchorman was the Holy See? And that's the way it is, all these decades later, can't get the haunt of them out of my nostrils; blowing doesn't do it, sneezing doesn't do it, even inhaling abrasive compounds doesn't do it.

As for my tactile sense, through which babies get the information that doesn't yet come through sight, I couldn't feel the silver spoon in my mouth. Because I wasn't born with one there. Nevertheless I felt the poignancy as Duchamp reflected on his readymades; they represented, for him, "a way of getting out of the exchangeability, the monetarization of the work of art." Not yet desperate about the ultimate futility of this gesture of Duchamp's, as many of us would be by the end of the century, I was merely touched, not yet tempted to make my own statement about it. I touched all the knick-knacks I could reach, knocking down a goodly percentage of them in the process by accident, but I can say this much in my defense: at least I didn't have my finger on a button simulated to control voltage, and didn't receive a dollar to prove that "Sixty-five Percent in Test Blindly Obey Order

to Inflict Pain." Some adults had their fingers on some very red buttons, poised to produce real pain.

I lost 10 ounces, I gained 12, and the first U.S. Polaris submarine arrived at Holy Loch. The stem of my umbilical cord went into a little box that went into a box a little less little, at the time that a ceasefire was struck in the Algerian War of Independence. Winnie's went at the same time. Irene didn't have Vaseline on hand to rub-a-dub-dub on the site of the lost stump, so Mother proposed to her the merits of a little dab of Brylcreem. The scab over the place of the missing umbilicus fell off prematurely and left an itch that can never be scratched. The old tube was replaced by a vacuum tube with a gun that never observed a ceasefire, an electron gun in a box my parents called the console. And we needed consolation: The USS Proteus was sent to refit Fleet Ballistic Missile submarines, that is, make of them nuclear weapons. As regards the TV, we needed Vaseline to soften the image, but we had run out.

A movie was made of *Voyage to the Bottom of the Sea*. But in real life, the Cold War notwithstanding, the Russians and Americans got together on the Cuss 1 to drill a hole in the bottom of the fucking sea. Who knows, maybe mineral research would eventually have led to better weather predictions, and even oil, but the project failed five years and fifty million dollars later. The Mohole Project made me wonder why anyone who had drawn breath after a nine-month tour of duty in a similar medium would want to reenlist. Holy Loch, Batman. Why, likewise, do the shrinks imagine that babies mind being thrust out of the womb, where it is dark and wet and cramped, and the senses are stunted? Fetuses everywhere scream — you scream, I scream, we all scream — for a large screen. But Winnie saw it differently. We argued the point while Mother and Irene quarreled about cigarettes.

Frank and Irene's dream came true in the form of Hilltop Steakhouse, for which they found prime real estate on Route 1. Under the crisp and yellow scotch tape on the wall, the first dollar bill — Dad's — probably still hangs, testament to the opportunities for young white people with entrepreneurial Yankee ingenuity, the budding lifelong friendship between Winnie's parents and mine, and the national passion for beef. Frank played proprietor while Irene played hostess. They worked seven days a week from early morning until late at night, and Irene was so bushed by the end of every long day, she would fall asleep on the stool while Frank finished cutting the meat for the next day. It's not easy to fall asleep on a stool. From the time that particular dollar bill bypassed the cash register, Winnie spent a lot more time with us.

Digests and weeklies paraded cultural developments: "Three Major Programs Show True Artistry." With Disney now presenting the Wonderful World of Color to us, Winnie and I could hardly disagree. Then again, we could hardly see. To inform our nascent taste buds, Mother read to us from "Exciting Television":

> The exhilaration of creativity came to television last week in three programs that for the moments of their magic stemmed the tide of lamentations over the state of the medium. Out of the overworked box in the parlor came electrifying excitement and beauty of art pursued and realized.

Earlier that day, we had heard the preacher on a tide

of Lamentations (whose authorship, incidentally, is also uncertain—was it one or was it many?), as though the very Temple were going down the drain of the cult of popularity. Now the Instantaneous Audimeter we had just received from Nielsen sat looking back at us through its single eye, watching us watch TV, or more precisely, listening to us change the channels as we voted for better and worse, or worse and worse, programs, according to taste. *Certainly I hope you will agree that ratings should have little influence where children are concerned. It used to be said that there were three great influences on a child: home, school and church. Today there is a fourth great influence, and you ladies and gentlemen control it. If parents, teachers and ministers conducted their responsibilities by following the ratings, children would have a steady diet of ice cream, school holidays and no Sunday school.* As television ascended, as the magic of its representations attained the status of art, as Mother and Dad considered changing churches, representational art took a hit. As though TV and the abstract expressionists were in cahoots. As we read in *Culture Guide*, ". . . it is certain that...there can be no individual in this

country more powerless than a nonabstract painter." Not counting the necessarily anonymous painters of print ads, who bemoaned their anonymity all the way to the bank. Winnie favored Punchy of Hawaiian Punch fame, while I preferred Charlie, the tuna who had good taste. Although we may have expressed our preferences in saliva, there was no doubt we knew what we liked. The likes of TV and representational art would redeem each other soon, they would more than cahoot, they would marry, and the baby in that manger? Thy name is Warhol.

If you think babies can't prefer things like that, you should think again. With all due respect. Being preverbal does not protect against the electronically transmitted. There is no prophylactic against the image; even looking away, even shutting your eyes, you're soaking in it. Why the prophets warned us about icons. And when images are mobilized in the service of profits, here come the holy ads, which

> . . . establish contact with the subconscious of the consumer below the word level. They do this with visual symbols instead of words... They communicate faster. They are more direct. There is no work, no mental effort. Their sole purpose is to create images and moods.

So said the guru of advertising, Rosser Reeves — the name is for real — in his masterwork, *Reality in Advertising.* A contradiction in terms? No, not at all. Warhol got the vibe. I got the vibe. The other baby pig in the blanket in her bunting got the vibe. We couldn't not.

The asymmetrical tonic neck reflex active in newborn humans is also known as the "fencing" reflex because of the characteristic position of the infant's arms and head, which resembles that of a classically trained fencer. When my face was turned to one side, the arm and leg on that side extended, and the arm and leg on the opposite side bent. Winnie, equally and oppositely, fought back. When the majority opinion of the Supreme Court ruled in Hoyt v. Florida that state laws that effectively excluded women from jury pools were not invidious discrimination, but rather, were an "inoffensive" attempt to accommodate the "special responsibilities" of women, and that women tried before the resulting all-male juries had no valid claims under the equal protection clause, my tonic labyrinthine reflex, which expresses itself orally, kicked in: *That sucks,* I thought, reflexively. A baby swordplayer, fancy footwork and all, positioned as though, but as yet unable, to say: *En garde.* Who will later point the same weapon, the rapier (plus a wit just like it), at the avant-garde. What did Winnie think about Hoyt v. Florida? Well, she wasn't born a woman; what girl is?

Anyway, from early on, she was all about the weapon.

That is known as a primitive reflex. Equally primitive is the step reflex, also called the "walking" or "dance" reflex, because a baby appears to take steps or dance when held upright with his/her feet touching a solid surface. Chubby Checker was speaking my language:

Now you turn to the left when I say gee,
You turn to the right when I say haw,
Now gee, ya ya little baby,
Now haw, ya oh baby, oh baby, pretty baby,
Do it baby, oh baby, oh baby,
Boogety, boogety, boogety, boogety shoo.

I clapped my gee-haw hands. To this tune, Winnie bopped, establishing, by her precocity, her girlhood.

In late April, pop king Elvis Presley topped the chart with "Surrender." At about the same time, French General Maurice Challe, who led the Algerian army rebels, did surrender. Although a referendum may have supported DeGaulle's Algerian policy earlier in 1961, three of his own generals, of which Challe was one, did not; they attempted a coup. They failed. Closer to home, the first so-called terrorist hijacking of a U.S. aircraft took place on May Day, when Antullo Ramirez Ortiz

held a National Airlines pilot at gunpoint, demanding to be taken to his haven in Havana. We learned this, my parents and I, on TV, where we had seen an episode of *The Dupont Show with June Allyson* called "The Haven" the month before. *Program materials should enlarge the horizons of the viewer, provide him with wholesome entertainment, afford helpful stimulation, and remind him of the responsibilities which the citizen has toward his society.*

These were my formative moments. In this, I was no different from anyone else, not even Winnie: the brain, my brain, was more plastic at three and four months than it would ever be again. I lay flat on my back, kicking my legs, my little baby urine soaking into my cloth diaper. By my parents' report, I spent a fair amount of time laughing at blank walls, pacified when distressed by the soothing sounds of the television. Winnie and I, like parallel sausages encased in our class, were rigged up next to each other so we could see too. *When television is good, nothing...is better. But when television is bad, nothing is worse. I invite you to sit down in front of your television set when your station goes on the air and stay there without a book, magazine, newspaper, profit-and-loss sheet or rating book to distract you — and keep your eyes glued to that set until the station signs off. I can assure you that you will observe a vast wasteland.* Imagine!

This is what was being said, unbeknownst to us, on May 9, 1961. Newton Minow, chair of the Federal Communications Commission, was saying it to the National Association of Broadcasters, elaborating on the violence and idiocy of the fare that the broadcasters had scheduled for people like us, invoking shit like *decency, decorum, propriety,* and *advancement of education and culture,* while a pack of admen and producers sitting in circles knocked their drinks over on the white tablecloths and jerked each other off underneath them. I'm talking about Exhibit C, in which Minow resounded like the Moses or Mohammed of his day: *The power of instantaneous sight*

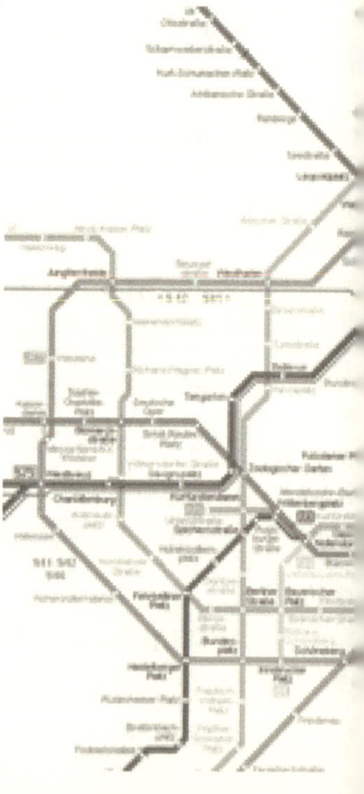

and sound is without precedent in mankind's history. This is an awesome power. The Audimeter blinked, as though God himself had shut off the power to criticize. *It has limitless capabilities for good — and for evil.* In effect, Minow called for a high art of television. Less magic, he might well have said,

> We need imagination in programming, not sterility; creativity, not imitation; experimentation, not conformity; excellence, not mediocrity. Television is filled with creative, imaginative people. You must strive to set them free.

History may have vindicated Fidel Castro, but it has not vindicated Minow, sounding an awful lot like a fellow Red here: *I urge you to put the people's airwaves to the service of the people and the cause of freedom.*

Thus concludes Minow's speech. I can't say I remember the occasion of its delivery. We couldn't have seen it, because it wasn't broadcast (except to broadcasters), but it was quoted like a motherfucker. If I may.

The concept of good television was like the fluoride in the water, imperceptible to the taste, yet contributing to the health of the national teeth. Or not. Nor do I

remember Kennedy making the rounds in Europe, meeting with DeGaulle in Paris, exactly as rebel generals Maurice Challe and André Zeller were sentenced to 15 years in prison. But in the sixties we did not underestimate the power of subliminal communication. I rolled over in my crib and Kennedy turned up in Vienna to talk with Khrushchev about Germany and nuclear testing and disarmament, or so the TV reported, though they must, in fact, have met not so much to agree to disagree as to perfect the art of talking without saying, subtext and lies like submarines swimming through the translation of their non-conversation. Memory swam just under the surface in optics, in physics, in chemistry, and in the literal water along with the fluoride.

Mother's Day, like most minor holidays, found us hydroplaning up to Saugus for dinner at Hilltop. Dad's treat. Mother's Day found Frank and Irene busier than usual, dads all over giving moms the break of steak. Anyone who's ever been on Route 1 would have noticed the steakhouse because of the big steer sculptures grazing on the grassphalt out front. Even after the Sinclair dinosaur and the Leaning Tower of Pizza went the way of all flesh, those cowboys kept at it. Meanwhile, away from the ranch, that very Mother's Day, civil rights struggles went into overdrive. Coincidently — but not incidentally — we ate at Hilltop, and Freedom Riders got off the bus for a pitstop only to be beaten by a mob in Alabama. Ten days later, they were arrested in Mississippi for disturbing the peace. Interpolated by the screaking populace, mothers all over the country ran down the checklist: hungry? tired? wet? sick? Yes, mothers of children, we are sick, sick at heart. Racism was not healthy for us and other living things.

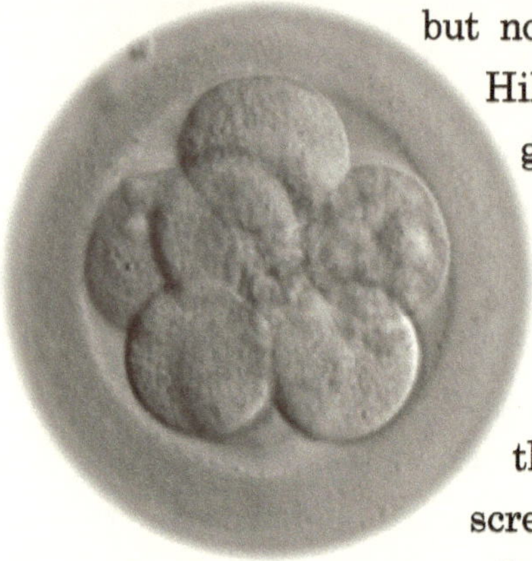

In a May 17 speech to the U.S. Senate, Senator Harry Flood Byrd disparaged the NAACP, stating that the organization was "more interested in the integration of public school children than it is in the education of colored children." He was speaking of Prince Edward County, in which public schools had already been closed for three years in an attempt to subvert a court order to desegregate (how's that for "contempt"); white adults there had arranged for private school participation for the community's white children. Figuring the NAACP as interfering "outsiders," Byrd described a threat to the well-being and tranquility of Prince Edwards County, whose white leaders had, after all, just that fall, arranged for the charity of an additional private school, this one for Black children. It received one application.

And was I not a child? Although illiteracy threatened to grow in at least one "black belt" community in which desegregation would be hung up in court for years to come, the literate rest of the country was reading *The Wretched of the Earth* and *To Kill a Mockingbird,* bemoaning the oppression of the colonized and plain old poor folks Black and otherwise, globally and locally, though it was never a problem in my backyard. And *The Moviegoer.* Moviegoers were seeing *Through a Glass Darkly* and *West Side Story*—catchy tunes, no? Winnie and I caught a few. In France, there was a new *Bible de Jerusalem,* and

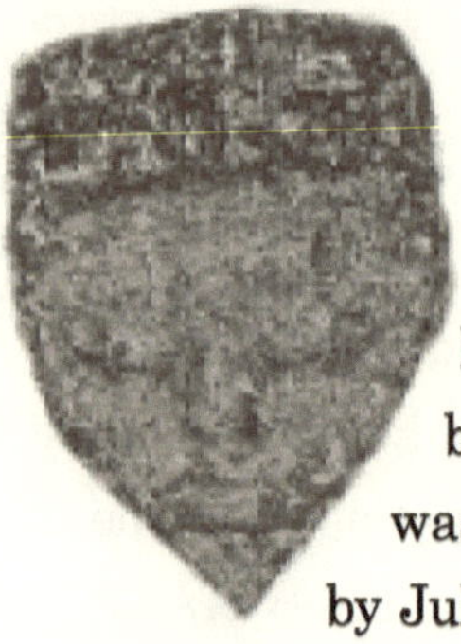

Eichmann was in Jerusalem too, but back in the States, Mother's new bible was *Mastering the Art of French Cooking*, by Julia Child. I was not that kind of Child. Nor was I a flower child.

Trujillo was shot dead by twelve guys on San Cristóbal Avenue, Santo Domingo, and Cristóbal Colón turned over in his grave as I turned over in my crib. Do we ever stop arriving in the New World? Do we ever stop passing the buck, evading our seeing-eye agency, having "no active part," in unending murders, and only a "faint connection" to the guilty parties? Not that Trujillo was some kind of peacenik, just that it becomes hard to tell the difference between U.S. and Them, when you know damn well that an internal CIA memo will later reveal that there was "quite extensive Agency involvement with the plotters" — fair-weather friends and elite paramilitary operations officers from the Special Activities Division.

Time-Life books began publication, both of which began to curl in on themselves, as did space. I rolled over and over. Kuwait became an emirate, bringing its status as a British protectorate to an end. But the British had already done all the damage necessary in the Middle East (necessary to ensure conflict in the region for decades to come), even before Mother and

Dad were born, around the time Mary Richardson did her thing in the National Gallery. But I anticipate. I anachronize. The narrator takes liberties, as might anyone who spent an ambigram in a pram, as predicted. Yes, I'm coming to the point. Ask my folks about 1961 and this is what they say: the baby came in January, they met their pinochle-partnering match, and steak was no longer out of their reach.

General Maxwell D. Taylor, second President of Lincoln Center for the Performing Arts, Inc., was recalled to active military duty on July 1, 1961. Just like I said he would be. He resigned his post in the art world ten days later, to become the military representative to President Kennedy. Your Honor, are you paying attention? Do I have to hand this to you on a silver platter? Because, where I've been staying, I've had a little trouble getting ahold of a silver platter that's not made of tin foil and pasted to the wall in place of a mirror. Having swung from one to

the other of the antipodes that bookended our little world, mine and Winnie's, General Taylor reengaged one way of performing arts. Of war. State of the arts of war. Are you getting the medium — because if you got the medium, you got the message. Winnie and I got the message, but we interpreted it differently. And even though a young actress was making a splash in *The Miracle Worker* on a stage of the kind Taylor had just left — making a name for herself and us — Winnie and I were still much too young to Patty Duke it out.

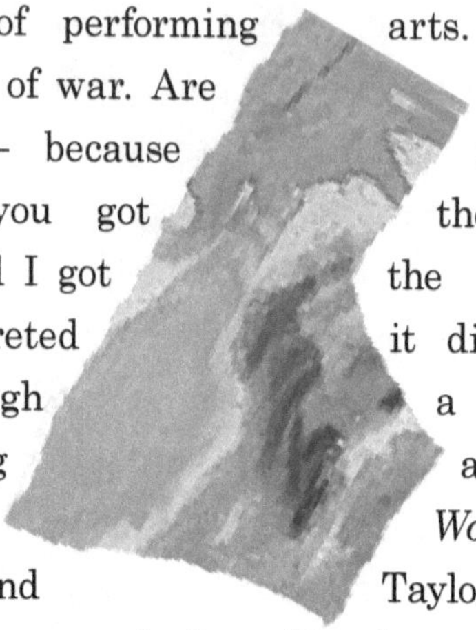

On my first Independence Day, baba in my hand, I watched with my parents the report of the Soviet submarine K19 exploding in the North Atlantic, but the balance of deterrence swung back the next day with the launch of the first Israeli rocket, Shavit 2, built by RAFAEL Armament Development Authority for the purposes of meteorological research. More weather. All those half-truths were mother's milk to me. And Winnie too, and all the toothless young, north, south, east, and west. When we were eight months old, construction began on the Berlin wall, and soon thereafter, "You Must Have Been a Beautiful

Baby" debuted at 30, just under "Human," which was down from number 29 the previous week. As one, I was progressing. But Winnie was the beautiful baby — of that there was no doubt — with a smile that could charm a Navy SEAL.

Ontogenetically, I unfolded according to the script. A full set of primary teeth lies in wait beneath the cute gums of the newborn; at birth, those teeth are in the process of being calcified, and some of the permanent teeth are already in development too. The infrastructure and apparatus for taste are the sine qua non of social life. Newborns, with a curiously well-developed sense of taste, already like sweets, which is

why nursing infants sometimes refuse to nurse when they taste garlic or heavy spices in Mom's breast milk. For the bottle-fed generation, this is not a problem. But *I am not convinced that the people's taste is as low as some of you assume.* By 1961, there was a choice of commercial baby formulas available on the market. One aisle over from the freeze-dried food and the extruded edibles. Science in the service of mankind! Clean wholesome fare for our kids! For me! But was this really the order of the day? Minow's imprecations resounded, exhortations against commercial formulae on the boob tube:

> You will see a procession of game shows, violence, audience-participation shows, formula comedies about totally unbelievable families, blood and thunder, mayhem, violence, sadism, murder, western badmen, western good men, private eyes, gangsters, more violence and cartoons. And, endlessly, commercials — many screaming, cajoling and offending. And most of all, boredom.

As television violence became a category, the question of its effects became a question. So psychologists expounded the question by setting children to pounding on the famous Bobo doll. We all knew Bobo or knew someone who knew him, the clown with the sand bag in his bottom. Bobo who got knocked down but got back up again. Bobo, the clown with the sand bag in his bottom. Bobo who got knocked down but got back up again. That Bobo. Inflatable, indefatigable Bobo. Mass-produced Bobo. *The* Bobo. In the famous eponymous experiment, Albert Bandura sought to test whether children would imitate aggressive behavior modeled for them. Whereas psychologists had previously believed that seeing others vent aggression would drain a viewer's aggressive drive, Bandura concluded from the Bobo Doll Study that *exposure to modeled aggression is hardly cathartic.*

I submit Exhibit D. Watch with me while *The room contained varied play materials and children could choose to play aggressively or non-aggressively.* Watch with me while *Sockaroo. He sure is a tough fella. Kick him. Knock him down. Pow.* He gets knocked down, Bobo does, but he gets back up again. Bandura called it *the learning of aggressive styles of behavior through watching.* He had to conclude, *Sockaroo. He sure is a tough fella. Kick him. Knock him down. Pow.* At that point, it could have been no surprise that *Children also picked up the novel hostile language.* Look at how *The children devised new ways of hitting the doll.*

What did Bandura call it, *novel forms*, the great new ideas the kids got for bashing Bobo. See, *Here's a creative embellishment: a doll becomes a weapon of assault.* Bobos bouncing down and up all over the same vast wasteland where *There are some fine children's shows, but they are drowned out in the massive doses of cartoons, violence and more violence* as the Jolly Green Giant stomped around shouting "Ho Ho Ho," Winnie following suit, playing Bam Bam to my Pebbles, and HoJos went public. *Must these be your trademarks*?

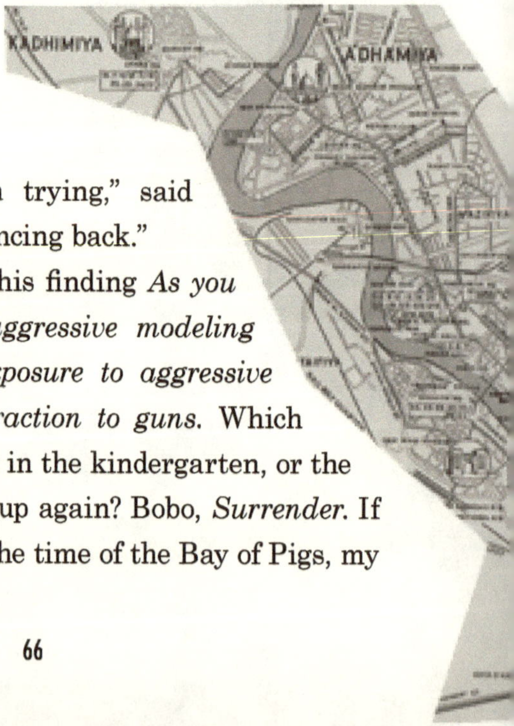

"Aggggressssion, Bobo," said Yogi.

"Give me a break," said Bobo.

"He-e-ey, Bobo, I'm trying," said Yogi. "But you keep bouncing back."

Bandura published his finding *As you can see, exposure to aggressive modeling is hardly cathartic. Exposure to aggressive modeling increased attraction to guns.* Which was worse, the brutality in the kindergarten, or the fact that Bobo got back up again? Bobo, *Surrender.* If I had not let go of it by the time of the Bay of Pigs, my grasp reflex certainly wore off when the Organization of Atlantic States slipped an anti-de Gaulle message into French TV programming. De Gaulle was slipping too. On October 17, the French police attacked 30,000 protesters who were demonstrating against a curfew for Algerians. I could no longer get what was being said under the din of what was not. Please make room for Exhibit E, which is what Time magazine said about the massacre:

> Jostling into the Place de la Concorde, the Etoile, the Place de l'Opéra, the Champs Elysées, and half a dozen other Paris landmarks, tens of thousands of Algerians came swarming from slums and shantytowns to protest a new 8:30 p.m. curfew that applies only to Moslems.
>
> Chanting *Algérie algérienne*, the demonstrators at first shuffled peacefully by in the rain. But at the Rond-point de la Défense, just outside Neuilly, the rabble borrowed its tactics from French extremists in Algiers and Oran: slashing tires, overturning cars, shattering shop windows. Shots rang out and police, flailing night sticks and heavily weighted capes, clashed headlong with the mob.
>
> As fast as they could catch them, police and security troops hauled the Algerians off to improvised detention centers, including a psychiatric hospital. At week's end, 15,000 had been

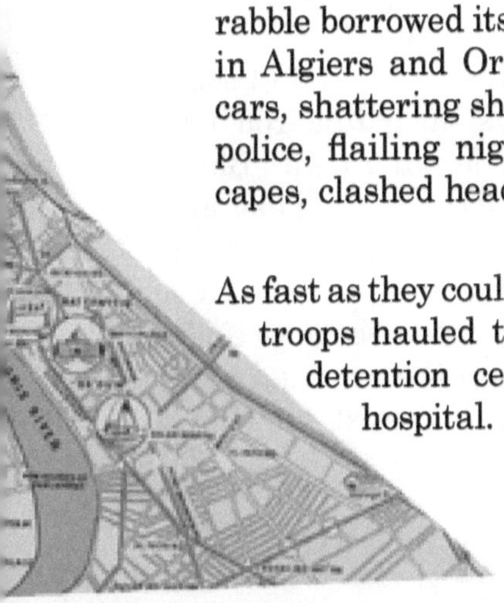

> bagged for what officials bragged was “the highest number of individual arrests ever made by the Paris police.”

What *Time* magazine did *not* say: under the instructions of Prefect Maurice Papon, who had established his expertise in the surveillance, roundup and “processing” of minority populations as a functionary of the Vichy government, the French police instigated and then responded to Algerian protest with deadly force. Exhibit F:

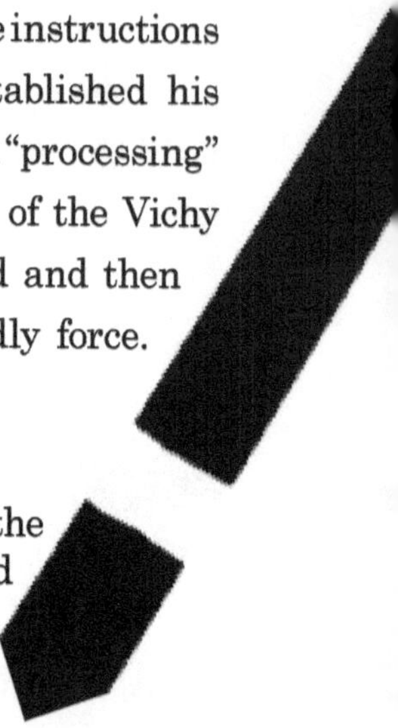

> Although witnesses report that the demonstrations were orderly, and conducted with inexpressible dignity, the police lined up a cordon of men in front of the bridge [Saint-Michel], and at the juncture with the boulevard Saint-Germain, trapped hundreds of Algerians in a pincer movement and then attacked with great violence.

> [P]olice wielded riot clubs, rifle butts, and in some instances, “unofficial weapons,” including iron bars and pick-axe handles, with lethal intent. Blows were aimed with maximum force at the head and stomach, and as hundreds of Algerians arrived in hospital casualty wards doctors catalogued a discernible pattern of injury: open scalp wounds, cracked skulls, broken bones of the arm and hand that resulted from attempts to ward off blows,

> internal damage to the stomach and intestines and broken legs. So savage was the onslaught that thirty of the fifty clubs issued by police district commander Mézière were broken.

Who knew, besides the intestines in question? Talk about your *non-dit*! As living Algerians climbed out of the Seine, the dead waited to be pulled out of it. *And forthwith found salvation in surrender.* Where shall we file this exhibit, Your Honor? On the walls of what institution should this shit hang? The Pentagon? The academy? The church? Don't say museum. Don't it hang, even now, dripping green blood, by the still-sticky adhesive to the George Washington my Dad exchanged for cow parts? At the Steakhouse, summer business had dropped off, so Frank and Irene had the TV on at the corner of the bar, and Winnie, still the precocious one of us, began to cruise from stool to stool. She babbled up a storm; sometimes it sounded like she was saying *Got you got you.* I had the gift of no language and my first French fry.

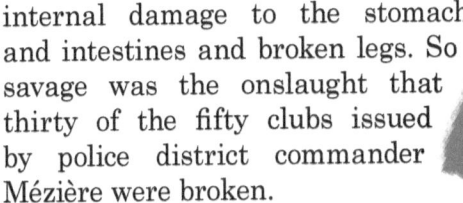

The French fry of the Algerians reminds me of A.C. de J., an otherwise unemployed Dutch guy, who walked into the Dordrechts Museum, and went on a two-minute slashing spree with a triple-bladed knife that he had made himself. He stabbed ten paintings by Dutch artists, an act he explained as a response to the influx of workers from other countries: "By letting all those foreigners live in our country, we are throwing away our Dutch culture — thus, there's no need for those paintings anymore." That's clearly offensive, though maybe it beats stabbing the foreigners themselves. Leave that to the state. But just so you know, the authorities let him go when he agreed to stay out of

Peking
Tientsin
Dairen
Tayuan
Langchow
Sian
Nanking
Chungking
Wuhan
(Hankow)
Shanghai
Foochow
Taipeh
TAIWAN
Amoy
Canton
Hong Kong
T-
M
Railways
Projected Railways (1961)
0
500 Miles

museums for the next six months. And later on, he hammered out a more constructive approach, representing, in his own work, in his own words, "the conflict between abstraction and realism."

But I say don't give the Dutch guys knives. Another one, also otherwise unemployed, made a pit stop at the

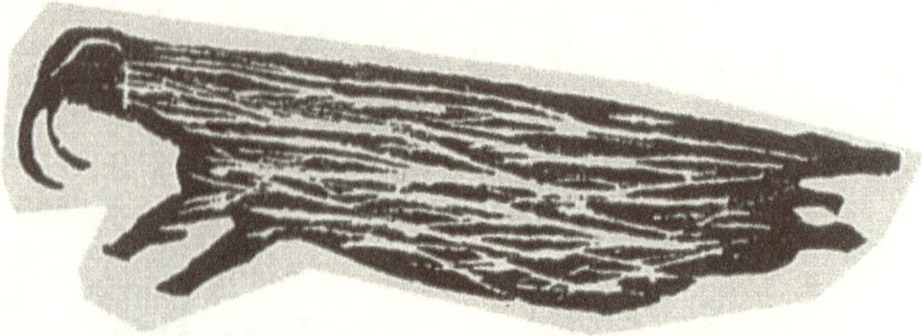

church where Rembrandt is buried, claiming to be the painter's son. When he was asked to leave the church (love it!), he went into the Rijksmuseum and slashed Rembrandt's *The Night Watch.* Okay, fine, but he had been sent by the Lord, forced to do it by "forces out of this Earth." That guy killed himself the next year. Lots and lots of them — or should I say "us" — are sent by the Lord, for the Lord, from the Lord. And offing yourself on top of it? That just supports the assumption that we're all crackers, but in every profession, you're going to get some unstable practitioners. Then again, it was an *American* with a knife, owner of a shoeshine stand, who

did up a Frankenthaler in Washington, D.C., a Joan Mitchell, a Gottlieb, a Philip Guston — Jesus, have you ever looked at Guston's work? Probably made that picture prettier. But why? To denounce the anti-Christ in Europe: that was why he wrote in red crayon "Antichrist Ronald Reagan 666." If that's trenchant social critique, it's just an accident; I happen to agree with his assessment, but I don't credit him with political purpose, as I do the reactionary Dutch guy.

Chicks with knives, now that's another story. The famous case, of course, is Mary Richardson — my all-time favorite — and I might have been right there with her, if I'd only been born. On March 10, 1914, dressed as an unassuming white woman in a trench coat, Mrs. Richardson broke out of her apparent contemplation of Velasquez's *Rokeby Venus*, pulled out the hatchet that had been concealed under the coat, smashed the glass protecting the painting, and began chopping. "Yes," she said to the guard who led her away, "I am a suffragette. You can get another

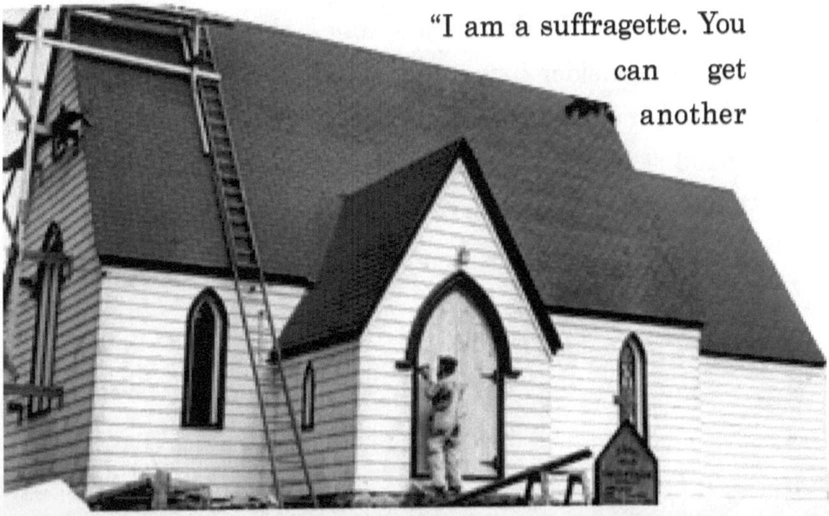

picture but you cannot get a life, as they are killing Mrs. Pankhurst." Indeed, Mrs. Pankhurst was on a hunger strike in prison at the time.

When he sentenced her to six months, the judge asked Mrs. Richardson if she knew that, "If the picture had been destroyed, no money would have replaced it?" A former art student whose concern for art had been replaced by her concern for justice, Richardson answered with this defense: "Do you realize that no money can replace Mrs. Pankhurst? I think it is a shame," she added, "that I had to consider it my duty to do it." Years later, she offered another insight into her attack on the painting: "I didn't like the way men visitors gaped at it all day long." But back in court, she had given this statement, Exhibit G:

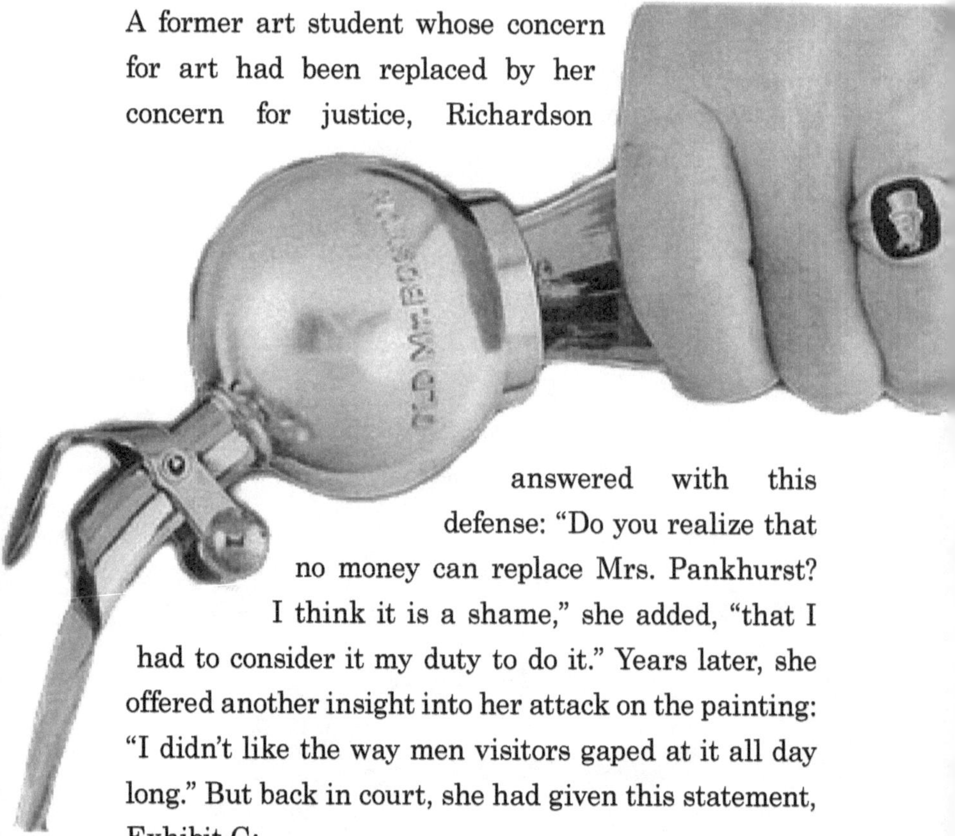

I have tried to destroy the picture of the most beautiful woman in mythological history as a protest against the Government for destroying Mrs. Pankhurst, who is the most beautiful character in modern history. Justice is an element of beauty as much as colour and outline on canvas. Mrs. Pankhurst seeks to procure justice for womanhood, and for this she is being slowly murdered by a Government of Iscariot politicians. If there is an outcry against my deed, let every one remember that such an outcry is an hypocrisy so long as they allow the destruction of Mrs. Pankhurst and other beautiful living women, and that until the public cease to countenance human destruction the stones cast against me for the destruction of this picture are each an evidence against them of artistic as well as moral and political humbug and hypocrisy.

Two days after the massacre in Paris, the last British troops left Kuwait as the Arab League took over Kuwait's protection. Two weeks later, the Soviet Union detonated Tsar Bomba — the mother of all bombs — a 58-megaton-yield hydrogen mother. It was the biggest explosion ever rigged by

Homo sapiens sapiens, and still is. Talk about your *rockets' red glare*, your *bombs bursting in air.* Talk about your *feu d'artifice.* I know, let's pretend it's aurora borealis, or or or — I know, I've got a good one, let's say it's a deterrent.

By the beginning of December, I started pulling myself up on my feet. Fidel Castro declared himself a Marxist-Leninist and declared Cuba communist. Red glare. I fell on my butt. The Marshall Plan expired. I pulled myself up again. The first American helicopters arrived in Saigon along with 400 U.S. personnel. I fell on my butt again. Portugal ceded Goa to India after 400 years of colonial rule. I pulled up. By the end of 1961, the world's population had reached 3 billion. Wow — that bowled me right over. Eichmann was pronounced guilty of putting a dent in that population figure — I pulled up — and was sentenced to death. I fell down. I pulled myself up, and I walked away from the TV, with the smell of Chetley and Humperdinck in my nostrils, but I could not get out of hearing range, no matter

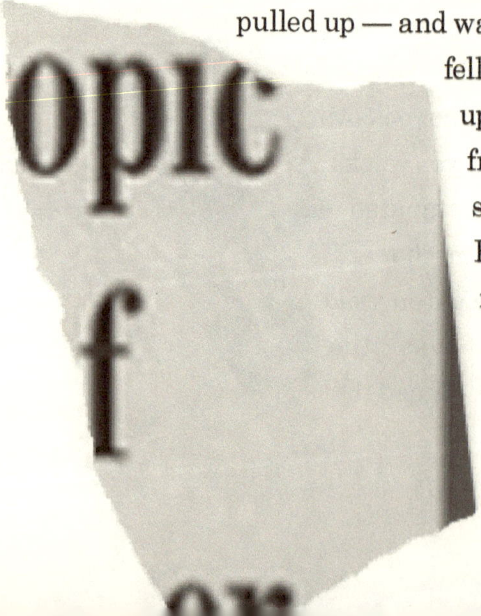

where in the little split-level house I went. American helicopters arrived in South Vietnam, with — guess what? — American personnel to fly and maintain them. The rest is history.

The rest is *the children could choose to play aggressively or non-aggressively, the learning of aggressive styles of behavior through watching, novel hostile remarks: pummeled a doll with a mallet,* pummeled Bobo with a doll, *he's a tough fella, flung it in the air, kicked it repeatedly, threw it down and beat it.* The snow began to fall and everything was new. According to ratings, Mother and Dad and Frank and Irene voted for Harry Belafonte singing "Swing Dat Hammer." Hell of a spectacle, but not no Nouveau Realism. Al Minns and Leon James danced on the *Dupont Show of the Week*, but here's what was in the internal memos that Dupont did not make public: Teflon kills mice.

And know what else killed mice that year, and rats too? 2,4,5-trimethylaniline — more mothers' milk — covering more wasteland than *Ho ho ho.* 2,4,5 was a plant growth inhibitor and herbicide used to control sucker growth on tobacco, and it was applied to 30-40% of tobacco in the USA. It was also approved for use on beans, beets, citrus fruits, corn, lima beans, onions, peas, potatoes, strawberries, sugar beets and tomatoes, and for onion and garlic control in pasture land. Female and male rodents died differentially. Vive la.

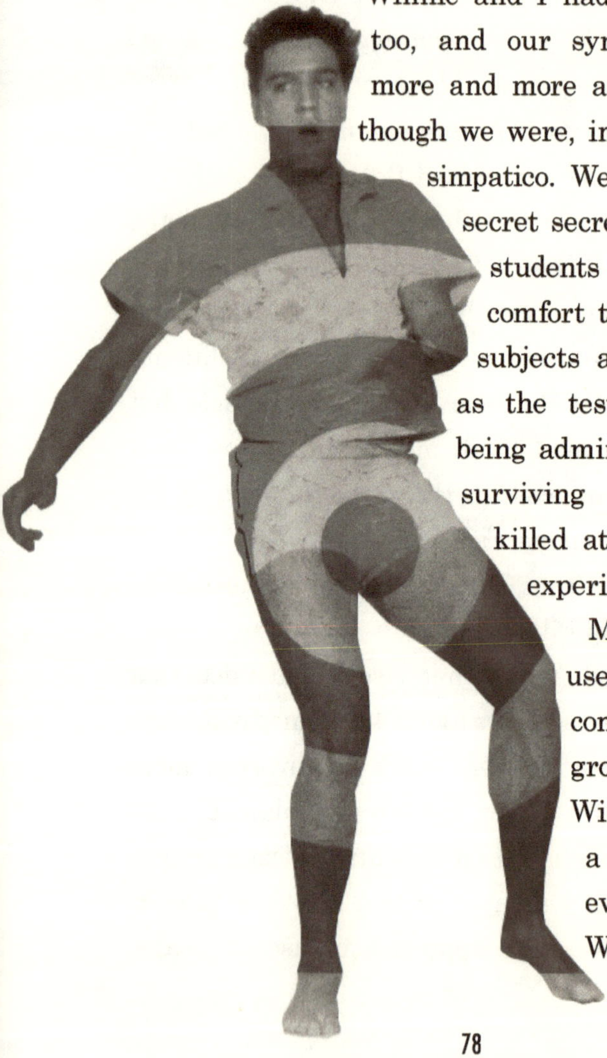

Winnie and I had our differences too, and our symptoms differed more and more as time went on, though we were, in so many ways, simpatico. We sucked on this secret secret: soft graduate students rushed in to comfort the experimental subjects at night as long as the test chemical was being administered, but all surviving animals were killed at the end of the experiment.

Mother and Irene used formula to control sucker growth in me and Winnie, but there's a new one born every minute. We didn't know much, but we knew what we liked. The Proceedings from the Flavor Chemistry Symposium explained why, but only to the peers who reviewed the 662 GRAS — Generally Recognized As Safe — flavorants that year. Their results were published by FEMA — no, not the emergency agency you think it is — the Flavor and Extract Manufacturers' Association. This is what was circulating in the collective bloodstream while the Algerian massacre was festering in the collective unconscious. The mind and the body of the whole damn polity. You are what you eat what you don't know you don't know won't kill you, but what you don't know you do know will. Sing a song of sixty-one: it was a fuck of a year.

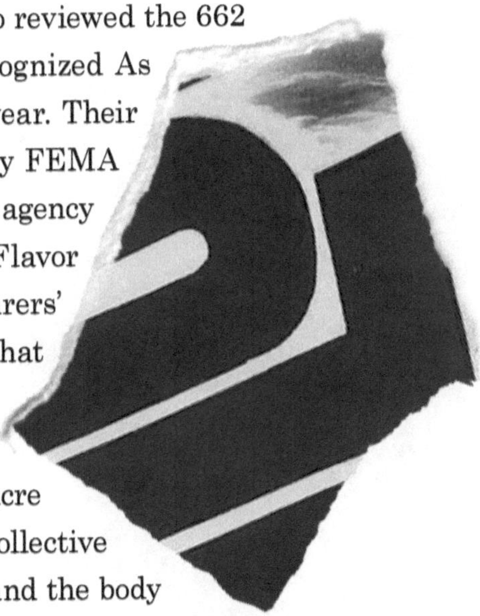

But I believe, and I hold this conviction where some people hold their *foi*...gras: a certain historical juncture is my chart, its events my signs, my houses and planets, my sun and moon, Walter Cronkite's voice my rising and falling — under the sign of Sputnik, and the ceiling of the Boston Lying-In Hospital, in the shadow of Brown v. Kansas Board of Education — I

was born a metal Rat on 13 Sh'vat, 5721, an Aquarius, in the dawning of the age of the same name. Make that two metal Rat Aquarii, myself and Winnie, who slurpeed up the same zeitgeist. We were determined to express it ontogenetically — I mean we had no choice. But goddamn it. Why did she have to be the one to go? And leave me.

Winnie was over at our house one-a-day and pulled herself up at the coffee table where the prior month's *Look* magazine lay open to a picture of a white boy and his beagle telling a photographer armed with a Polaroid, "Don't just stand there, do something." Shoot. Paralyzed by the TV, we watched "Missile Bound Yogi," the one where the army holds war games in a sealed-off section of Jellystone, which frightens Yogi into thinking the park has been invaded. One of the war-game teams dresses up as bears — art imitating life. Looking back now, I think this must have had a deep influence on Winnie; she wanted to dress up as a soldier dressed up as a cartoon bear. I got more

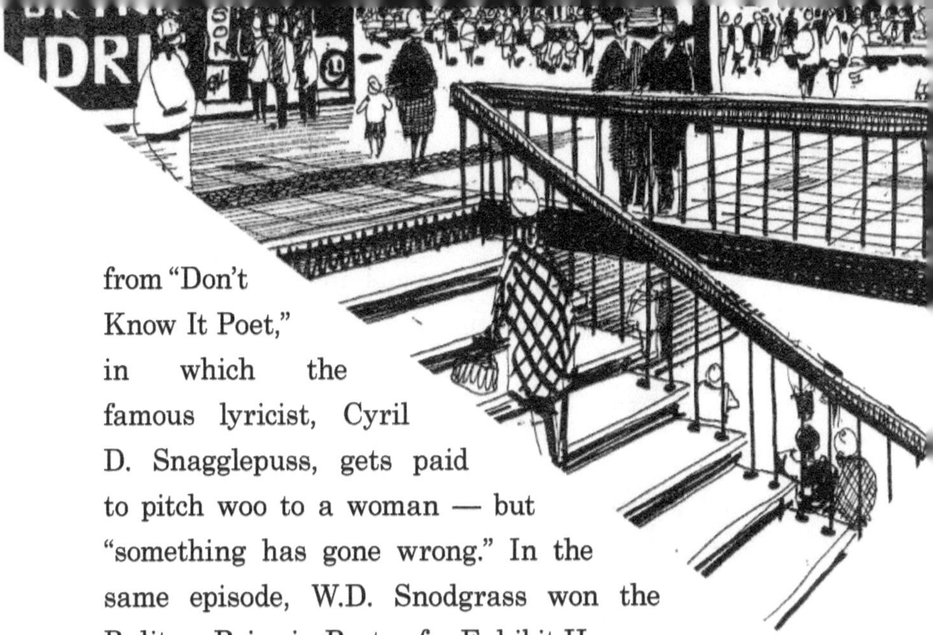

from "Don't Know It Poet," in which the famous lyricist, Cyril D. Snagglepuss, gets paid to pitch woo to a woman — but "something has gone wrong." In the same episode, W.D. Snodgrass won the Pulitzer Prize in Poetry for Exhibit H:

> Child of my winter, born
> When the new fallen soldiers froze
> In Asia's steep ravines and fouled the snows,
> When I was torn....

Oh no, that was real live poetry with the unhappy ending in which Winnie would be dressed up as a soldier for real, and even decorated. *Heart's Needle*, the name of the game to which she would turn between episodes of "The War." But I'm getting ahead of myself, in light of what came later.

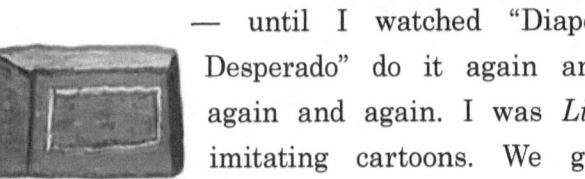

I hung back developmentally. I didn't have the psychological or motor skills to crawl away — until I watched "Diaper Desperado" do it again and again and again. I was *Life* imitating cartoons. We got instant mashed potatoes, spuds in a box, imagine the brilliant military applications. Fred and Wilma and Barney and Betty got sponsored by Welch's grape jelly. We got language from the telly. Which is to say, Rachel Carson's 1962 *Silent Spring* was my last. As my age-appropriate babble morphed into recognizable morphemes, and I put tongue to palate in service of the issue of "Mama," "Dada," "TV," *Webster's Third New International Dictionary* was published. It had an unprecedented 2,726 pages — 450,000 entries, of which I knew three, although I was mistaken about the meaning of *Dada*. Though criticized for its perceived linguistic permissiveness, the new dictionary took hold, becoming the reference work of all subsequent generations to date, loose, profane, authoritative. So perhaps we can be forgiven. For cultural

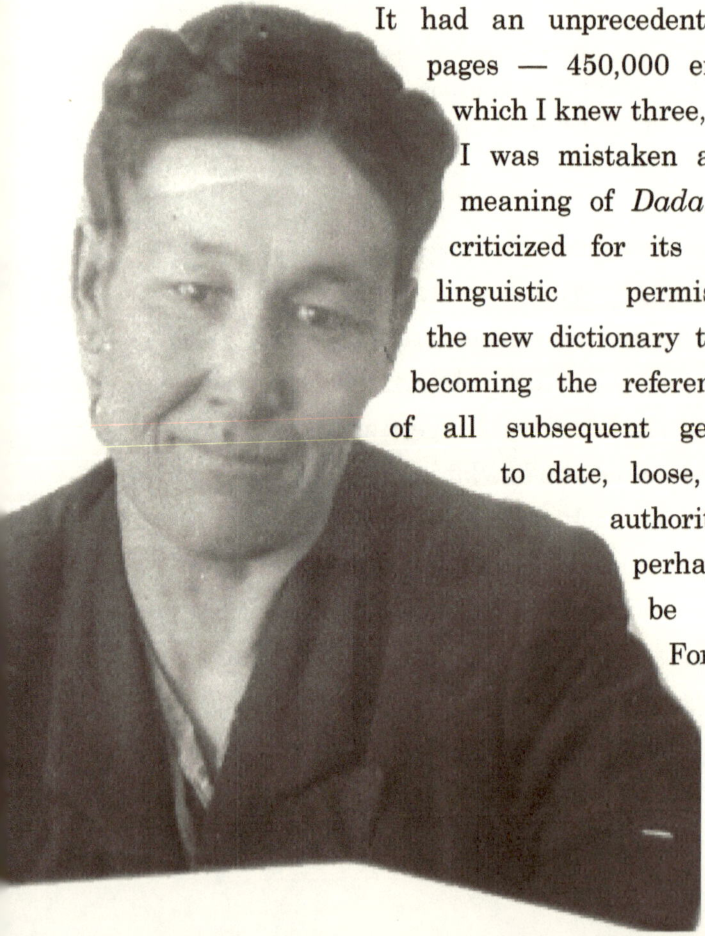

neologisms that may have ensued. High-brow hybridizing into low.

Blender recipes were all the rage. Mother just threw it all in there for supper, but she did learn something from Julia Child: she cut our collective mayonnaise consumption in half. Because just a dollop will do. Trust me: she was a fine mom. Cinnamon toast. Sweet. Dad flirted with smoking a pipe briefly; as briefly, he feigned style in the form of a hat. Hat and pipe have spent the rest of his life in boxes in the closet. So was I born this way, or was it the second-hand news and the muzak, foreshadowing that the times would be a-changing? Of course, the times had always been a-doing so, and still are, but it's not just the hand you're dealt, it's the start time of the game. For our first birthdays, Winnie's and mine, Mother and Irene baked and frosted a moist cake from yet another dry box; the dads hoisted us up on their shoulders, noisemaker *bwaa*, the vanilla festivities bland against the snowscape, blackout, fear, and the empty boxes beginning to make a drop in the bucket of the landfill.

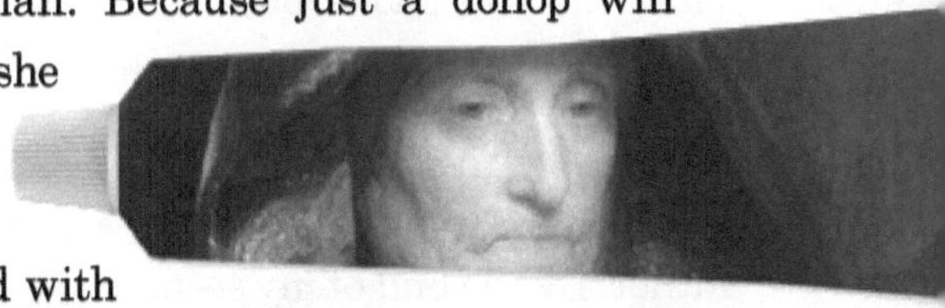

The decreased plasticity of the brain of a child at

one year of age meant Winnie and I would never learn so much again in a single year, not even in a decade. Our channels had been set though our bodies would continue to grow in more ways than twelve. But no matter how many vitamins you choke back, suck, or chew, the best predictor of adult height is the family history — the height of one's mother and father. By the end of my second year, my height reflected my genetic heritage. As did my race and sex, which is typical, according to what they say. Ready, set, go: there was the race for the moon. Race and sex: *Another Country, West Side Story,* to name two. The soundtrack of the latter topped the charts for over a year: "Cheap-o, commie gitme goo," Winnie and I would take turns shooting and being shot.

So maybe the question isn't why would I vandalize a great work of art. Maybe the question is: Why wouldn't I strap on an AK 47, stride rite into a

McDonald's, a high school, my office, or any public place without a metal detector eating the front door, and open fire? Why would I not head straight for the orange uniform of today, just another one of the growing millions and billlions and trilllllions of global wastrels fed on the golden calf under the arches of the same hue? Why wouldn't I issue, in blasts, my manifesto for equal access to those commodities, both sides of the bars of the box, called taste and choice and Taster's Choice? Why didn't I star in my own video, webpage, fanzine, intra-active collage, in a flak jacket and dilated pupils? How did I become, instead, Inqui, the Destroyer?

And when? At the very moment that Arman came to the U.S.? He was the French artist who had already established his reputation as a great artiste with his *Poubelles (Garbage)* and his talents for *Accumulations* (same in French and English, same almost everywhere but the Trobriand Islands). He was doing his "destruction" thing, which had him cutting and burning and smushing things on canvas. Smushitti. Still on the canvas.

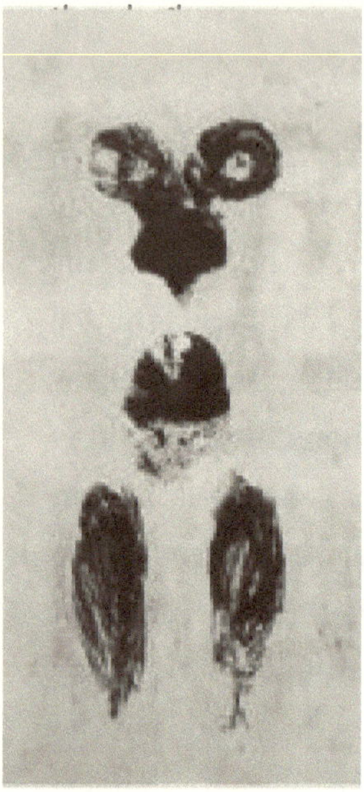

Meanwhile, on the glass canvas where all colors were black and white, and all brushstrokes dots, Snagglepuss got a job as a television actor, but the job was harder than he'd imagined, so a couple of episodes later, he tried his hand at Shakespeare — with Major Minor hiding in plain sight in the audience. Yakky's sick singing formed the plot of one show, hitting the airwaves about the time of the second annual Once Festival, venue for avant-garde music and the cutting-edge integration of sound environments into music, perhaps paving the way for once and future cutters across media, like Arman, and like William Burroughs, who

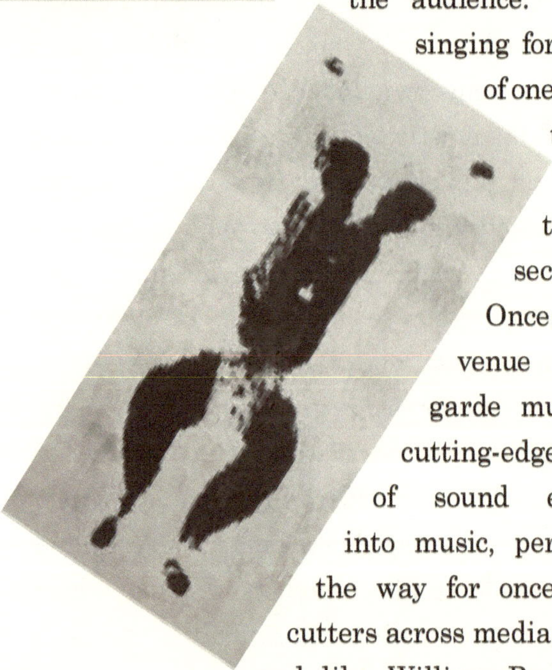

would be cutting up soon himself, between injections. Classics in the offing. Major Winnie and Minor me, not appreciably smarter than the average bear, imbibed a lot of Yogi, since his Hour of airtime fell within our parents' weekly social dates. We both became Yogi, though in very different ways, always trying to get away with something, outthinking the ranger on patrol.

Consider, Your Honor, that it takes brains to beat out the security guard who, in only seconds, will have made his or her way across the museum gallery to apprehend, for example, an attacker intent on making mincemeat out of a Lichtenstein. Did you see this in the news recently? *Classic of the New*, a three-month exhibition of the American pop artist's work at the Kunsthaus Bregenz in western Austria, had been as

uneventful as any retrospective when, on the final day of the show, a 35-year-old woman pulled a knife from a handbag and did the deed to *Nude in Mirror*. I totally relate; you stand there looking at it, unable to get out of the *mise-en-abyme*. Talk about No Comment.

Cloaked in custody, said assailant said, "I know I shouldn't beat myself up about it." But I'd like to see her try. So why did she do it? She was convinced that the painting was a fake. Not that Lichtensein was a fake, nor all paintings ever painted — that's what's so funny. Originally the museum hoped to keep the vandalism secret,

because, according to the museum's press spokesman, "Museums are always afraid that this kind of publicity may encourage other acts of vandalism." The offender faced charges for grave property damage, and for scratching and biting the police officer who relieved the security guard on the scene. *I* never scratched or bit anybody, did I? Also, she had to get some psychiatric attention, and we all know what that's like. Charges can be beat or sentences can be served, but four foot-long slashes still scar the painting, which was insured anyway. You've got to admit, nudes can be very provocative.

Winnie used to tell a story about her first and last day of Art History at the academy. Watch with me while time curls back on itself... again. Showing a slide of Manet's *Olympia*, Winnie's professor asked the students to describe it. Having noted all the features so commonly noted, like the white whore's brazen gaze outward, the brushstrokes, the Black servant bearing flowers, the composition and the lighting, Winnie added, "Oh and she's naked," just in case there was nothing so obvious that it wouldn't earn her credit to mention. "In Art History," replied the professor, "we call it 'nude.'" Like you'd have to go to school to learn to say *nude*,

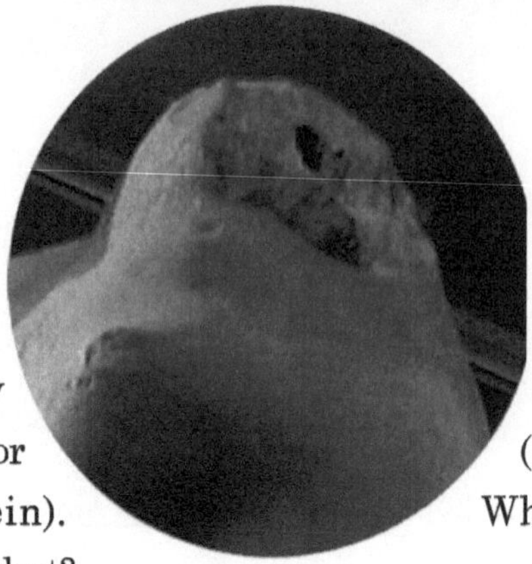

though you'd seen it every day of your life in the mirror (unlike Lichtenstein). What the fake is up with that?

This has been an ongoing issue in art vandal history. Not long ago, in an attempt to highlight the injustice of criminalizing public nakedness (not nudity), one vandal painted a large dollar sign in yellow paint over Rembrandt's *Self-Portrait at the Age of 63.* Wearing a dress, the vandal attached the tubes of paint to his thighs with rubber bands and waited over fifteen minutes in front of his work before painting over it. What does public nakedness have to do with money? The $64,000 question.

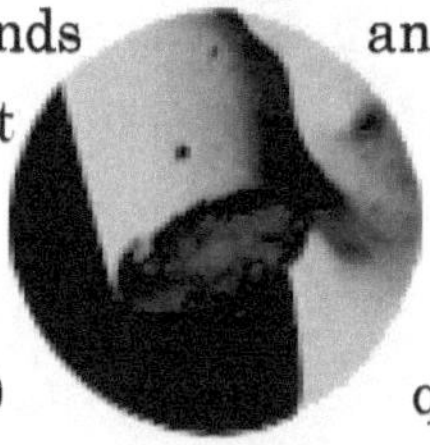

The answer: What doesn't? The National Gallery in London hushes up this incident — their files on it are still classified — because they don't want to give anyone ideas. Try getting any information from the Stedlijk in Amsterdam on the two times that paintings by Barnett Newman were attacked. They don't want to give anyone ideas. The museums don't. That irony flexes my muscles. Twitch.

Speaking of which, how about the German guy who attacked Barnett Newman's *Who's Afraid of Red, Yellow and Blue IV*? Josef Kleer was the first person in his family to go to college; on a break from his studies in veterinary medicine, he stumbled into the Nationalgalerie, where he noticed the reverential postures of his fellow visitors, which reminded him of the worshippers of the golden calf. When Kleer asked about the painting, a guard told him, "If it cost three million D M, then it must be art indeed." It frightened him, Kleer later said, and the painting represented an irresponsible use of public funds, and artists made too much money. So he placed a red catalogue of remedies in front of the red part, a yellow book in front of the yellow part, and a magazine with Margaret Thatcher conquering the Falkland Islands against a blue background on the blue part, then slashed the painting with one of the plastic barriers that held the public at a distance from the work — there it is, the irony — and left a handwritten note that said, among other things, "Whoever does not yet understand it must pay for it." Proof that "...beauty offends inferior beings who are conscious of their inferiority..." or critique of the claim? Or both.

So where do all these vandals get their ideas? The

homeless man who threw a stone at Mona Lisa because he was cold and broke and had nowhere to go? "Suddenly the idea to throw it came to my mind," but he came into the museum with a stone in his pocket. Where did I, Inqui, get my ideas? For all the insight and the x-rays, the professionals somehow failed to reveal, in the phrenological portrait of my skull, the frontal boxes that filled up in utero with Adlai Stevenson and other

Underdogs, and the smaller cells that filled up over the course of the next couple of years with T for Tiparillos, U the Unique Selling Proposition, the unanswered questions of, V the vindication of Vanzetti (U can't say the same for Sacco), and W the *War Requiem* (composed by Benjamin Britten for the reconsecration of Coventry Cathedral and performed by Dudley Do-Right), Ex-

Lax, Yogi, eternally Yogi, and Ze'ev Zrizi. One plus *One Day in the Life of Ivan Denisovitch.*

Call and respond to me through the windows of my incarceration — my eyes, through which, history — the horizontal holes doubling the sensory power of the waxy double helixes on the sides of my head, through which, the events of the world as told on the transistor radios as on the nightly news. Meanwhile, outside of the ticky-tacky televisual box, Frank Stella used Benjamin Moore exterior house paint to picture, to picture, um, to represent, vertical hold. No, even if I had one, innie or outie, I don't imagine my kid could do that. But the child I once and future was heard "Baa Baa Black Sheep" with increasing frequency, noted that "Twinkle Twinkle" had an identical tune, and then watched as the two morphed into the one and only "Alphabet Song." Does anybody remember vertical hold? Bars marching right to left to right, faster, slower, s l o w e r stop.

As African independence blossomed like a tin of Jiffy Pop, as Burundi, Rwanda, Uganda popped, E-Z Pop sued Jiffy for patent infringement and won, and Jiffy appealed and won. And as "exciting" television and faster color Kodachrome ran together, who could tell the difference between the life-size dunes on the screen in *Lawrence of Arabia* and "a method of direct appropriation of reality, equivalent, in the terms used by Pierre Restany, to a 'poetic recycling of urban, industrial and advertising reality.'" Thus, and then, the Nouveaux Réalistes advocated a return to "reality"

in opposition to the lyricism of abstract painting. They also wanted to avoid what they saw as the traps of figurative art, which was seen as either petty-bourgeois or Stalinist. Hence the Nouveaux Réalistes

used exterior objects to give an account of the reality of their time. And their tiempo was our tiempo. Meanwhile, the haute bourgeoisie earned dividends as predicted in the "Outlook for the Dollar," as delivered at the Insurance Forum by Walter B. Wriston, but we couldn't hear his forecast, drowned out, as it was, by the cries of the crowd for one Sonny Liston.

I toddled out of my room one night, and down the hall, catching my parents in the middle of what they did night-in night-out although they had tried to convince me that nothing ever happened after I went to sleep. I paused at the end of the wall that gave on to the living room, and peered in sideways, like a periscope, so that only the top of my head would be visible, should one of my parents happen to look up from what I knew must most truly absorb them or they wouldn't seem so ardent in their attempt to persuade me I was too young to see it, and then I saw it: slaughter. No need to ask was he hurting her. He was, they were, shooting their hoses like machine

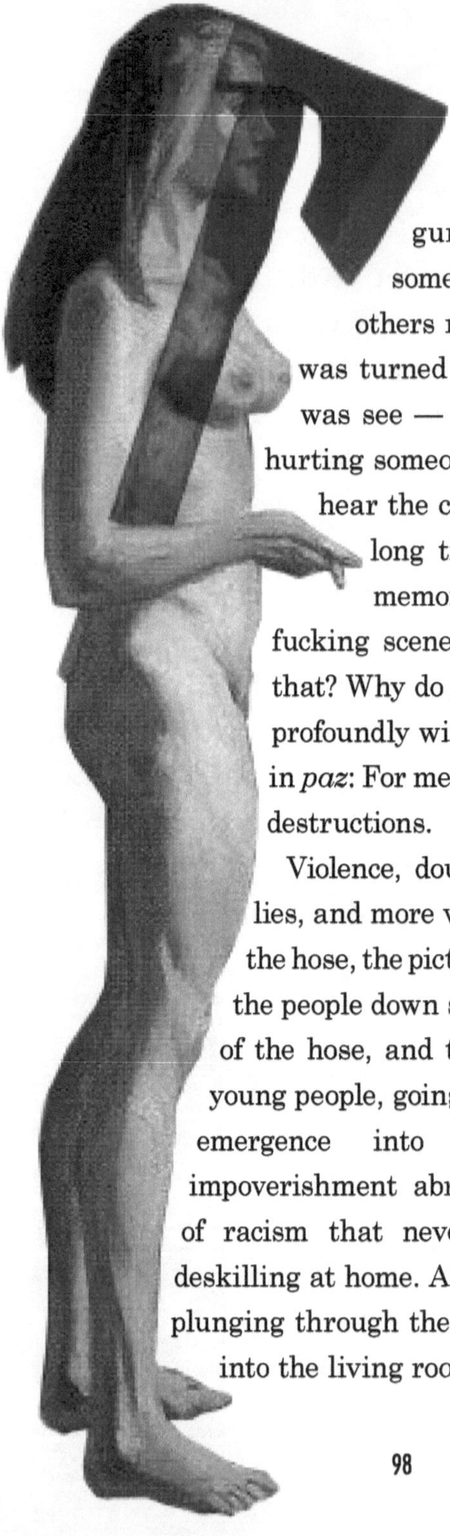

guns at dogs, at people; some were falling down, others rushing in. The volume was turned down so all I could do was see — certainly someone was hurting someone else, but I could not hear the cries of the fallen. For a long time, this was my first memory ever, my primal fucking scene. They got therapy for that? Why do you think I resonate so profoundly with Picasso, may he rest in *paz*: For me, an image is the sum of destructions.

Violence, doublespeak and outright lies, and more violence. I can't get over the hose, the picture of the hose aimed at the people down south, the silent sounds of the hose, and the sight of the people, young people, going down. Fear, mistrust, emergence into full-fledged modern impoverishment abroad, the illegalization of racism that never knew law anyway, deskilling at home. And killing. And all of it plunging through the cathode ray tube, shot into the living room — the most effective delivery system ever invented, subcutaneous got nothing on subliminal and subconscious. Information and Missing In (lights, camera) Action, and Smile, You're on Why do you think they call it dope?

Dope=intelligence=counterintelligence. The Cold War heated up. Major Popov had already popped off, courtesy of the Soviets who had possibly been tipped off by a double agent. Or possibly not. But now came others. Fedora. Chickadee. Do these codenames ring a bell? They must have rung Winnie's bell. Exhibit I is from a recently declassified document originally created July 20, 1962:

> CHICKADEE. Most recent reports were received July 4th and 5th, together with information leading us to believe CHICKADEE is in trouble. We conclude he is under suspicion, possible surveillance, and even might have been compromised to the point where he could be acting as a counter-agent. We therefore are studying his most recent reports which covered certain aspects of military doctrine most carefully, checking them against all sources available to us and are not disseminating them for judgment as to their bona fides.

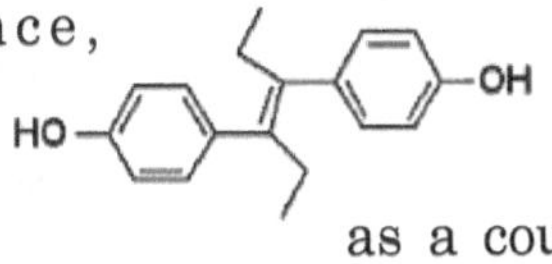

I got your bona fides right here. Remember Anatoliy

Golitsyn and Yuri Nosenko? Nosenko claimed to have interviewed Lee Harvey Oswald for the KGB, and rejected him on the grounds that Oswald wasn't "intelligence" enough to be an agent for them. Turned out Nosenko was full of unintelligible nonsense, and not just because he spoke Russian. He was lying, but all the surveillance in the world couldn't put Nosenko's story back together again.

They called me *Dr. No,* which came out when Winnie and I were two. Was I so terrible? No. "No" was normal for my age. Now, the captioneers call me the "Museum Masher," and they wonder why, what could possess a person to do the things I've done. Why, they wonder, am I incapable of watching an entire television show from beginning to end; why must I change channels as soon as I've arrived at a show I like, possessed by the fear that I might be missing an even better show that began four, five, six, seven minutes before? Why at 23 past every half hour do I throw the remote against the wall? Why do I bungee jump without a helmet? Why are my pipe dreams pyramidal? Why do I have eczema, sebhorrea, and psoriasis, scratching so loud the specialists can hear it in the next room?

When the journalists came during visiting hours to interview me, they left perplexed. I don't fit the profile: polite, church-going, quiet, secretive. I don't reveal a troubled past. I don't reveal at all, however freely I speak of my influences, or should I say symptoms? But which is the symptom, which the disease? Which is the vomit, which the museum? Why art, they kept asking: if I wanted to vandalize, why not do it to cars or people or other institutions? Is it random? Hell "no." Because art, that's why, the art of all of the above.And I never meant to hurt anyone. It looks like the journalists can write, but can they read...the signs? What must they forget in order not to know? *Ship of Fools* was published, but I could not read. Nonetheless, I could grok *The Gutenberg Galaxy,* which explained everything. Coincidentally, the first international communication satellite, Telstar, transmitted an image across the Atlantic Ocean — the wonderful world of colored bars. Which were mostly invisible — up until the very last

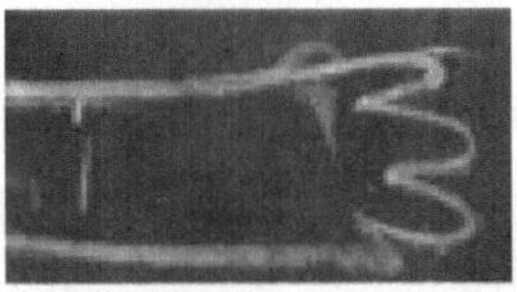

For Stewart from Robert
On the Day Jan 20 1961

DEDICATION

Summoning artists to participate
In the august occasions of the state
Seems something for us all to celebrate.
This day is for my cause a day of days,
And his be poetry's old-fashioned praise
Who was the first to think of such a thing.
This tibute verse to be his own I bring
Is about the new order of the ages
That in the Latin of the founding sages
God nodded His approval of as good.
So much those sages knew and understood
(The mighty four of them were Washington,
John Adams, Jefferson, and Madison) -
So much they saw as consecrated seers
They must have seen how in two hundred years

minute. The color-barred race-war cold-war race to me sitting there in that "lounge" watching "The Best of Reality" with a bunch of droolers.

I suppose I was a drooler once myself. From where I lay in my crib, the fraction of cloudy sky I could see out the window was criss-crossed by myriad sloping and slooping wires and lines, punctuated by poles. Clouds totaled into gray and spilled over into rain and everything was in fluxus. I thought I heard the plea for a new strategy for social contact as I lay in and out of it, the rising up against the lies of the divisions and subdivisions of our officially desegregated neighborhoods and of our branches of art and knowledge. I bleated, and when I was pricked, I bled. Just because we  were flushing sentimentalism down the porcelain pig, opening up to the nascent notion of concept and "concept art" — an art-form which is not sentimental, which is about metasyntactical dissociation, dialectical ingenuity, derivational process — didn't mean we had no feeling. Algeria voted for itself. Righteous satisfaction was tempered by an unspoken attack after the fact in Oran. Relief became bas-relief. Baa baa black feet fled Algeria and influxed into France.

When Winnie and I turned two, our Babinskis wore off: no longer would our big toes reflexively bend back toward the tops of our feet when firmly stroked. No longer would our other toes fan out. But Winnie would fan out, running moves under her breath, hiding behind the sofa making little bombing sounds. She was hardly surprised when she saw Jack Ruby shoot

Lee Harvey Oswald. It was the first time any of us had seen a murder on TV, which was itself just a lucky coincidence, but Winnie didn't even flinch. The cameras ran, Ruby shot and was shot; he got on TV. *Note to self,* thought Winnie. I practiced a different kind of fanning, through the fan magazines that Mom brought home from time to time. I was rooting for the Algerians.

Winnie and I differed on Ayn Rand too. I used *The Virtue of Selfishness* as a booster seat so I could reach my food. Winnie used it as a pillow to feed her head. Her ethical egoism would grow grandiose twelve wondrous ways over time, but for the moment, her nationalism nacreated silently on the North Shore, as Mother brought tainted French food to the table. Julia Child did not pronounce on politics, but she could sure pronounce *bourgignon,* which she now did on TV. From the book alone, you could not be sure how to say the names of the dishes. Malawi and Zambia gained independence. I stood on the front lawn freshly crew-cut by my dad. It looked just like the neighbor's lawn, and a lot like Frank and Irene's. Our houses looked similar too, though not identical. Surely each of us felt something unique relative to a genetically unique bit of suburban landscape.

Winnie and I would watch the cartoon landscape go by behind the animated chase scenes on TV, that landscape rendered as a series of repeating stills, so the speeding cartoon figure sped past the same

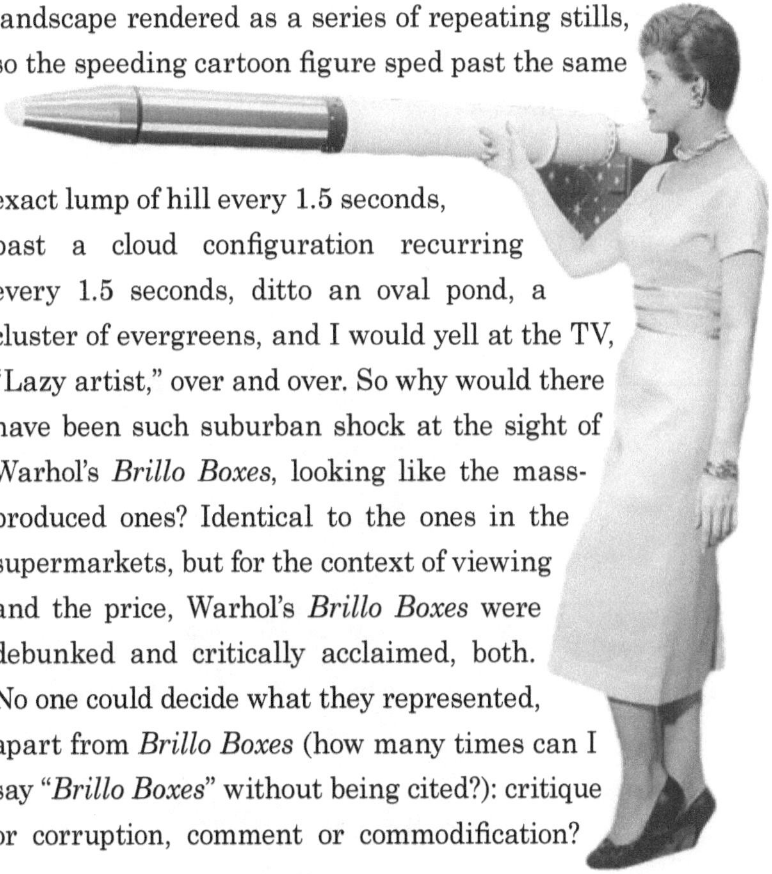

exact lump of hill every 1.5 seconds, past a cloud configuration recurring every 1.5 seconds, ditto an oval pond, a cluster of evergreens, and I would yell at the TV, "Lazy artist," over and over. So why would there have been such suburban shock at the sight of Warhol's *Brillo Boxes,* looking like the mass-produced ones? Identical to the ones in the supermarkets, but for the context of viewing and the price, Warhol's *Brillo Boxes* were debunked and critically acclaimed, both. No one could decide what they represented, apart from *Brillo Boxes* (how many times can I say "*Brillo Boxes*" without being cited?): critique or corruption, comment or commodification?

Or was Warhol just a lazy artist? Even now we do not know with certainty. Back in the day, or early evening, when my parents could pry us off the box in the living room, and cart us off to Hilltop, Winnie and I would run through the sprinklers while Frank and Irene pounded out the surf and turf.

Here comes AstroTurf. Have I mentioned that time began to curl back on itself? *Yeah, round around 'n up 'n down we go again.* As our growing and learning decelerated, time itself accelerated. The British Invasion and the War on Poverty were metaphors, but it was hard not to wonder bread all over again, and the New York World's Fair was anything but. But. There!

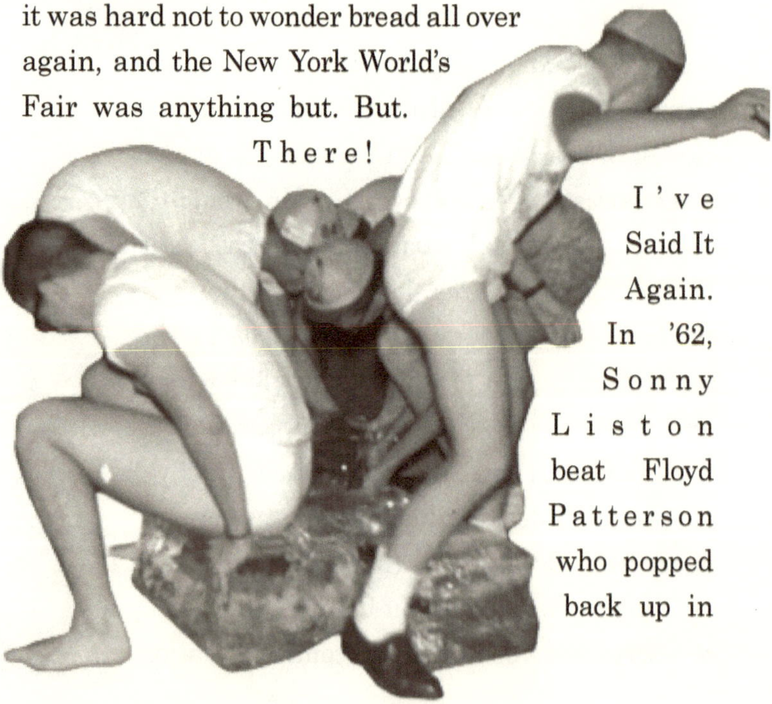

I've Said It Again. In '62, Sonny Liston beat Floyd Patterson who popped back up in

'63, when Liston knocked him down again. In '64, Cassius Clay beat Liston who popped back up again only to be knocked down in '65 by Muhammad Ali. I try to drum up a phrase that will sum up the sounds of silence echoing in the battered brain of the TKO. *Six, seven, eight, nine....* I've known that before it's come and it's gone/For all that it's been it's never been very long/What always seems to come is the sounds of silence. The Voice of Firestone's opera and classical music show went from radio to TV and bounced like rubber on and off that air for over a decade until it went off for good in 1963. There! I've never said it again, like The Whisper said, *Never again.* Not this time. But. Then Bobo bounced back up again in 1965, as he had in 1963. *Let's twist again, twistin' time is here.*

New protocol every couple of years, additional questions, refined objectives that only Bobo could probe. Bobo with a twist — what if children were to see a Bobo torturer rewarded or punished? Would that change their responses? Sure. Only children who saw the Bobo torturers punished did not imitate their behavior. Models who were treated neutrally, or who were rewarded, the children imitated: *Sockaroo. He sure is a tough fella. Kick him. Knock him down. Pow.* May I refer you back to Exhibit E. Watch with me while *The room contained varied play materials and children could choose to play aggressively or non-aggressively.* Watch with me while *Sockaroo. He sure is a tough fella. Kick him. Knock him down. Pow.* He gets knocked down, Bobo does, but he gets back up again. Bandura called it *the learning of aggressive styles of behavior through watching.* He had to conclude, *Sockaroo. He sure is a tough fella. Kick him. Knock him down. Pow.* At that point, it could have been no surprise that *Children also picked up the novel hostile language.* Look at how *The children devised new ways of hitting the doll.* What did Bandura call it, *novel forms,* the great new ideas the kids got for bashing Bobo. See, *Here's a creative embellishment: a doll becomes a weapon of assault.* Bandura published his finding *As you can see, exposure to aggressive modeling is hardly cathartic. Exposure to aggressive*

modeling increased attraction to guns. I want a loud answer to this question: "Who's your favorite clown?" Bozo asked as he took another bow.

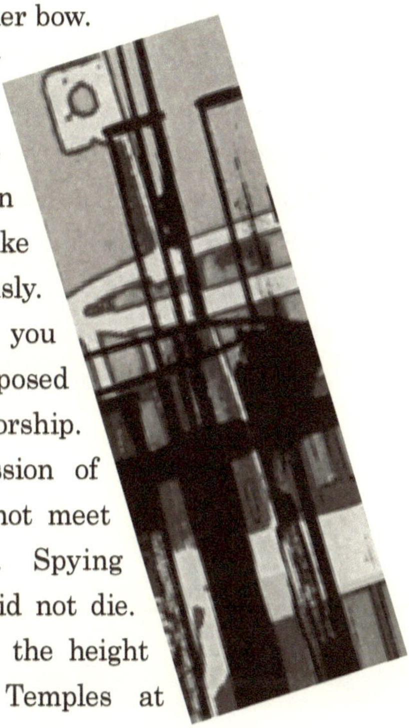

I believe in the gravity of my own particular sector of the New Frontier. There will be times perhaps when you will consider that I take myself or my job too seriously. Frankly, I don't care if you do. I am unalterably opposed to governmental censorship. There will be no suppression of programming which does not meet with bureaucratic tastes. Spying went underground but it did not die. Finally, Winnie and I met the height requirement for Shirley Temples at Hilltop. We learned new words every time we got taller, and vice versa, but what was that click on the line? Gambia, independence gained. Birthday party at the home of another child in our neighborhood, and through my first-ever glass of orange soda, Winnie, framed in its warped round bottom, still out in the backyard not yet having come in for soda, and using the birthday girl's new Raggedy Ann to beat the

crap out of her new Bobo doll. Winnie, why? Milgram thought it might have something to do with Obedience to Authority, as explained in his eponymous book; all those subjects who obeyed the command to inflict pretend pain on the people on the other side of the one-way mirror made him think so. Back in the year of *The Misfits*, when Sierra Leone and Iraqi pop star Kathem al Saher and Sweetarts and Winnie and I were born. Followed by all those media massages lodged beneath the threshold of consciousness commanding us to objectify and pummel each other. Why not just come inside and try the Fizzy Fantasmatic? It's dee-licious.

Time began to curve back in on itself. *The Battle of Algiers* came out, "documenting" events in Algiers from 1954 (cf. Vietnam. Coincidence? I think not) to 1960 (the month before I was born. Coincidence? Definitely not — it was a full month earlier). Are you following? I'm not. I'm barging ahead with the reenactment. The film begins and ends from the point of view of Ali La Pointe, played by Brahim Hadjaj, who corresponds to the historical figure of the same name. Yacef Saadi plays a fictionalized version of himself while Colonel Mathieu is a composite of several counterinsurgency figures, including a French actor who lost several jobs for condemning the actions of the French in Algeria. The author-actor-character had served in a paratroop regiment in Indochina as well as in the French Resistance during World War II, "thus giving his character an autobiographical element."

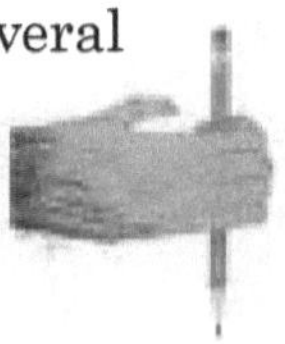

We were told that the film was in the style of a Documentary; we read that the film was in the mode of Realism, we heard that the film was an example of Verité. We did not know if we agreed. Though it was nominated for three Academy Awards including Best Screenplay, the film produced considerable political controversy in France and, like the truth about the Algerian massacre in Paris, was banned there for five years. Scenes of torture were cut from the original American and British releases as they were seen as incendiary toward the French. Except in classes on counterinsurgency — Winnie would years later report having seen the film again in one of her classes at the military academy.

We have to start from scratch with Ali La Pointe — flashback — getting his head bashed in — flashback — in front of Monoprix, shots from behind bars, call and response from behind bars, humane considerations can only lead to despair. "We have two faces. One smiles, the other cries." Operation Champagne, à la Marie Antoinette, singing "Hasta Mañana" in a bar that is about to blow is blowing has just blown up up up and away in my beautiful balloon. Dressing up and hiding behind mobilizing women hiding bombs in their womanly habits.

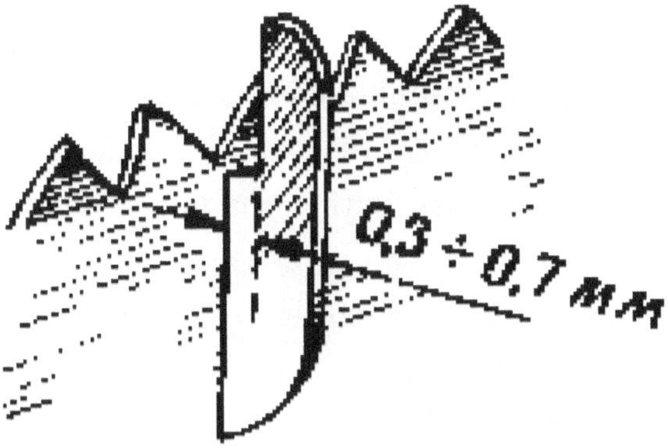

"C'est terminé le spectacle?"

"Yes, before it has the opposite effect."

"Humane considerations can only lead to despair."

"Couldn't you have talked sooner?"

"Get him dressed."

"What's the news from Paris?"

"Another article from Sartre."

"Why are the Sartres always born on the other side?"

"Analphabète."

"Original tactics."

The password: "We have two faces. One smiles,

the other cries." We have to start from scratch from start. We have to scratch from Sartre. We have to start from Sartre. Humane considerations can only lead to despair. Couldn't you have novel hostile remarks? Yes, dressed up as simulated targets before it has the opposite effect. What's the news from flung it in the air, pummeled a doll with a mallet. Vichy kicked it repeatedly, Vichy threw it down and beat it. Novel forms. Nominative: the most creative manifestation, a doll becomes a weapon of assault.

We used to play this game. Radio plays: golden oldies from before our time. Radio plays: non-segmented, not-yet-niche-marketed but non-classical music we call for lack of a better word Rock-and-Roll. Radio plays: Muzak. Muzak's 15-minute Stimulus Progression sound packages control how we feel and we don't even notice it. Muzak in the background soothes us and makes us more productive, less likely to haul off and hit people we're stuck in an elevator with in the foreground. Radio says: Use Crest toothpaste. Radio says: Use Rembrandt toothpaste. Use a Rembrandt as an ironing board. You lose. Duchamp said that.

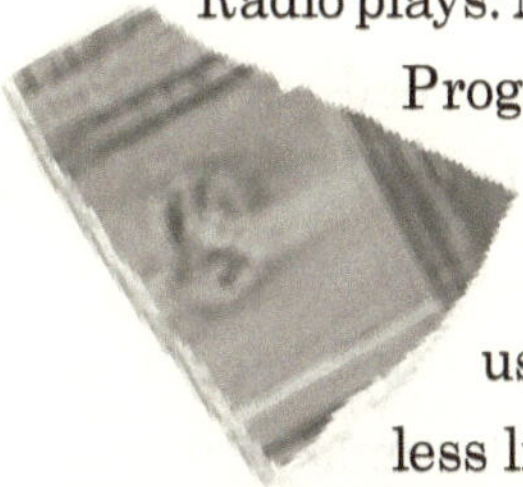

Red Rover Red Rover, in 1966, Botswana and Lesotho came over. In 1967, the Corporation for Public Broadcasting was established too little too late and with not enough money to stand up against the monolith of private broadcasting. 1968 found us slouching toward Trinitron. Rocketships took Silly Putty to the Moon by 1968, courtesy of the Apollo 8 astronauts. Equatorial Guinea, from a distance. Mauritius, Swaziland. Remote *en avant* le remote. There were, at some point, 200 million TV sets in the world, 78 million in the U.S. That's when Andy Warhol and Sonny Liston starred in a Braniff commercial. Warhol points at Liston, saying,

"Of course, remember, there's an inherent beauty in soup cans that Michelangelo could not have imagined existed." Liston appears to humor him just barely, as though he had had the misfortune to be seated next to Warhol by the randomness of seat assignments, and Warhol drones on but is soon drowned out by the voiceover's assertion that these celebrities fly Braniff because "They like our girls."

That's when, if not how, Rosemary had her Baby, and maybe the devil made her do it, but maybe it was all those red M&Ms. We watched the prices and the hem lengths go up — after all, if you got it, flaunt it — Winnie and I, as we worked our way through latency toward the impervious immunity of pre-adolescence. Sixty-six, -seven, -eight, -nine. Along with the end of the colonial era, the end of "Star Trek," the suspense had crumbled: Guinea-Bissau, Libya. No more surprises that science could not replicate. Or had documented or been documented by the lead-up to the moment of the reflections upon the Moon Walk the Woodstock the Future Shock the Moon Walk. Spiro Agnew broke our TV being so ugly, all the king's horses, only Charles Manson could put it together again.

I'm sorry, Your Honor, I became emotional. I'm in full control; I'm just getting into the story. Yes, I will try to leave off with the antics and come to the pointe.

8 МАРТА - МЕЖДУНАРОДНЫЙ ЖЕНСКИЙ ДЕНЬ

It's just, like it's all the years it's ever been, rightside-up, upside-down, 1961 rollover again. I find myself angry, as I have been so many times before, as though on Winnie's behalf, as though she had been caught up like a piece of polyester in the workings of giant gears, and then again angry *at* her, as I remember that she would have spurned the anger I felt as though on her behalf. I think grandiosity goes with the gig; it is part of the headgear for a Protean protagonist, a modern Mephistopheles, a talking headline. I know what you're thinking: Hitler was an unsuccessful painter. But am I really so bad? Is that the *non-dit* bouncing around your mind? Your Honor, I'm no Hitler, no Cortés, no Taliban, no Hun. I am just a lone individual with too many ideas per capita. Before, during, and after being

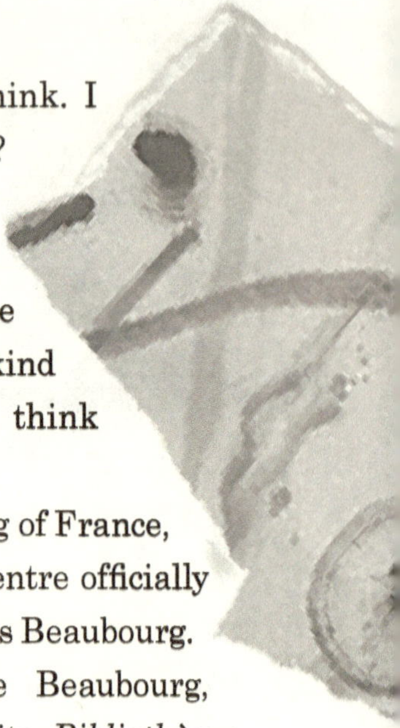

out on bail, a person has time to think. I think: What kind of sociopath am I? Then I respond intrapathically: the kind that patheth for normal until the dimensions of the box inside the head exceed the cranial capacity, the kind that surpatheth underthtanding. I think therefore I think back.

While Georges Pompidou was King of France, in 1969, construction began on the Centre officially named for him, known affectionately as Beaubourg. Mon petit Bobo. Hey, Booboo. Le Beaubourg, revolutionizing "the museum," with its *Bibliothèque publique d'information*, would open on our birthday in 1977. There and then, the work of Arman, the aforementioned Frenchie, now in his native land, went on show. But back in 1969, eight years before Arman opened in the just-opened Centre Pompidou, I caught, one day, a glimpse of Winnie in her soixante-leotard. It was then and there that my postmodern condition kicked in — nostalgia would precede memory — though it would be another eight years until I would kiss that girl.

The same year, the so-called Colossal Keepsake

Corporation deposited one hell of a piece of public art and information on the Yale campus. I heard about Claes Oldenburg's *Lipstick* on the radio. Women had been officially admitted to Yale that year, just in time for the arrival of the unofficial phallic symbol and literal platform for rallies, protests, posters and graffiti. Looking more than a little bit like a military tank, *Lipstick* was a guerilla gift for the up-and-coming second generation of New Leftists. And the administration was up in arms over the sculpture, ambivalent, no doubt, about the thing, given their ambivalence about the drama played out on it, their indubitably unalterable opposition to censorship warring with the materiality — the arms, that is — of the Black Panthers. Like spying, weather had gone underground, where comrades issued their "Declaration of a State of War." Meanwhile, secret security stood around above ground appearing to study the bushes, exposing themselves by sweltering in their serge suits.

On top of op, art became action, happening, event, everywhere, so that it was hard to tell the simulation from the real thing. Coke is, that way. Prisoner #8612 told other prisoners, "You can't leave. You can't quit." #1037 seemed to believe him: "I was told that I couldn't quit and at that point I felt that well it was really a

prison and at that point...um I don't know I guess there's no way I can describe how I felt I just felt totally hopeless. More hopeless than I've ever felt before." The guards began to act brutally, really "getting into" the "role." #416 said, "...it was a prison to me; it still is a prison to me. I don't regard it as an experiment or a simulation because it was a prison run by psychologists instead of run by the state." So how do you think the prisoners there regarded Attica, the realness "prison" really run by the state. Just like the white middle-class male students at Stanford, but so very different, they felt like breaking out.

Then, on May 21, 1972, a geologist named Laszlo Toth entered Saint Peter's Basilica and, approaching Michelangelo's *Pietà*, pulled a hammer from his clothing, and pummeled the famous sculpture while shouting, "I am Jesus Christ!" Was there an inherent beauty in his act that Michelangelo could not have imagined existed? Toth explained further: "Today is my 33rd birthday, the day when Christ died. For that reason, I smashed the *Pietà* today. I did it because the mother of God

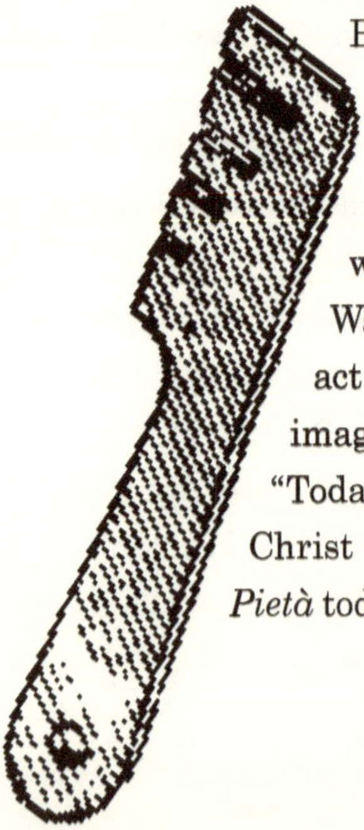

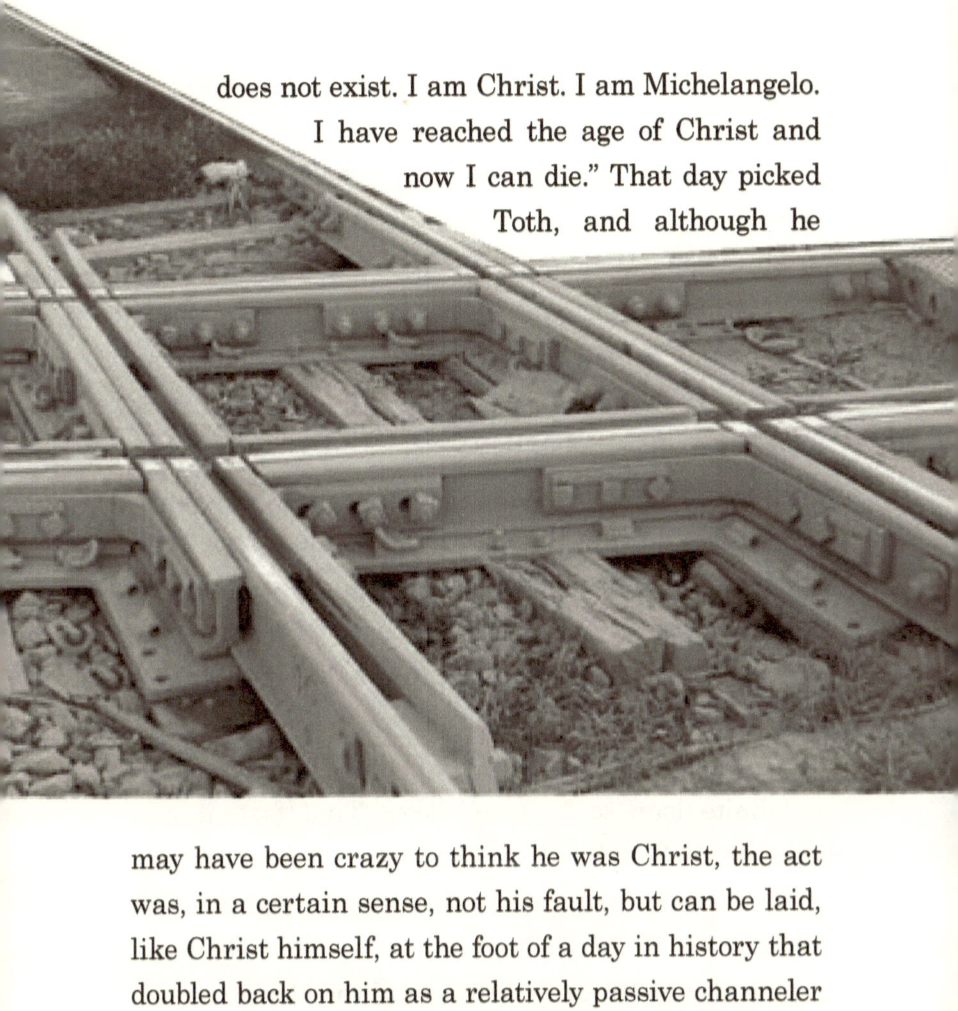

does not exist. I am Christ. I am Michelangelo. I have reached the age of Christ and now I can die." That day picked Toth, and although he may have been crazy to think he was Christ, the act was, in a certain sense, not his fault, but can be laid, like Christ himself, at the foot of a day in history that doubled back on him as a relatively passive channeler of time. In the end, Toth was found insane and thus was not charged with criminal offenses. And you never heard from him again, did you, except in the pages of a little gem by Don Novello, who tarred Bebe Rebozo with the same brush. Mon petit Bebe. Bozo again?

Anyway, I think you see the point I'm making, no need to beat it into the ground.

Winnie thought Toth should get the death penalty; she had begun to say stuff like that. I heard the echoes of Moses and Mohammed in those remarks, but they disturbed me nonetheless. She smiled when I pointed out the implication that art mattered. She didn't say yes, but she didn't say no. Oldenburg took *Lipstick* back from its unofficial installation on the Yale campus, but within a year, a group of art professors and historians organized to bring the outsized sculpture back from Oldenburg as an important work of American art. *Then conquer we must, when our cause it is just.* Money was raised to restore the sculpture and construct new steel tracks for it. In the fall of 1974 *Lipstick* was officially accepted by the Art Gallery and placed on indefinite loan to Morse College. That fast, it was canonized. *Now it catches the gleam of the morning's first beam. O say can you see* why I set my sights on the Ivy League, and I studied. I studied and studied and studied, swimming like hell toward the idea of college, forsaking sports and deferring drugs. Watergate, right? And I think there was an energy crisis. I came up for air only long enough to do a stint on a show sponsored by Giant Foods called *It's Academic*, which was my English teacher's idea, and which won me some scholarship money to a very fancy private prep school, where I would be able to study some more.

Mother and Dad kept on playing the hands they were dealt. Yogurt was invented, and sweetened for the American palette, while something like a Cuisinart was discovered in Europe, brought to the New World,

and adapted for consumption American style. The middle class jogged in jogging suits, cultured dairy products sloshing along in our bellies, catalyzing national health. Mother flirted with macramé and découpage. Dad hunched over, blowing little schooners into bottles, and then he reclined with some aching sciatica, and opined about the state of the world. The prevailing opinion at the fancy prep school was that there were only two things that offered redemption from the bourgeois hell in whose belly we lived: art and cocaine. My classmates hunched over, blowing big yachts right up their noses. Cocaine was not an option for me: although it clearly extended available study hours, it was expensive and seemed to make people nasty. So it would have to be art. Unfortunately, I couldn't draw my way out of a paper bag, so I decided I was an abstract painter, redemption squared, the ticket out of the television. Then again, maybe I would be a collagist, put the paper bags out of which I could not draw my way to work for expressly political purposes. Meanwhile, Frank and Irene put Winnie to work. She wasn't exactly hostess material, and they had these crazy child-labor laws back then, so she supervised deliveries of cow corpses in the back. Now that I no longer went to school with her, I saw her mostly on weekends, or whenever we went up to Hilltop.

Winnie was no longer exactly a child; she outgrew that condition before I did, although she was born later, and one day, the inevitable happened. With my parents inside at a booth, Winnie asked me to come out back behind the restaurant with her so she could have a smoke. She'd come a long way from baby. As she

fished in her apron for matches, I reached over and took the unlit cigarette out of her mouth, leaned in to her, and kissed her. I knew for a moment that everything I had ever known or guessed was true, and that everything unspoken could be said in not words. It was like being the most unsurprised I could possibly be. She pulled back and smiled the one smile. And then she leaned toward me and kissed me back. I went to pull her closer to me, but got caught in the pocket of her apron, so while I was there, I pulled out the matches she had been hunting for. "What are you?" she said. "Some kind of artful dodger?" That was it. She couldn't be with me because because because. We were too similar, too much like family, our families much too straight, our parents would freak. And I knew that everything she knew or could guess was right too. I knew I was no Romeo. I kept the smile, though I never touched her lips again.

While I was applying to every blue-blooded institution from here to Heaven, someone applied red lipstick to a sad white monochrome painting by Jo Baer in the Oxford Museum of Modern Art — it "looked so cold. I only kissed it to cheer it up," she said. Turns out there's a raft of possible applications of lipstick. And there's a whole tradition of folks adding color to art works they consider dull. That's when you get your primary colors flying through the air. Tradition? In that fancy-assed school, I studied art and art history. Somewhere in that milieu, that métier, that trade, I knew, I would make my living. Most kids my age applied to college randomly, or as directed by their parents who were directed in turn by instrumentality: their kids should want to go to, and soon get into, the best schools, bag the best possible jobs, and should, in the process, bring honor to the family. I fancied that I had a mission and I pursued it, joining the debate club just in case it was not too late to beef up my extra-curricular record. My parents voted for a full scholarship, if I could get one, and if not, they would see what they could do, even if it meant not getting a second car or a third television. They just wanted me to be happy. As the culture of narcissism flourished around them, my parents finally realized that they wanted to be happy too, so even though they were, they tried therapy, but their therapist fired them.

Frank and Irene likewise supported Winnie's decision to apply to military academy. Maybe it would save her from the full blossoming of the trouble she evinced in occasionally slurred speech, sleeping in, and the introduction of cheesecake onto the menu at Hilltop. The day she was accepted to the Naval School, I tried to write her a letter explaining why she shouldn't go. But after "Dear Winnie," I had nothing left to say because I had already tried, *Winnie, the needles are disposable, not you!* and it was clear that she was made for the military and it for her. But for that sweet smile, the more and more infrequent flicker of curiosity about my more and more tortured paintings, my less and less subtle collages, and the historical facts and deep thoughts I spewed wherever I went.

I suppose that was the parting of the ways, a parting that seemed to repeat again and again. On graduation, pompous circumstance and parting, and again the day she flew to South America and I drove down to New Haven, *adios, auf wiedersehen, adieu.* I suppose I should have accepted our differences. And then there I was at college: there was studying to be done. College hammered the humor out of me; I entered my self-serious period. I studied and I studied, dropping the studio for the library, the art practice for

the Art History. My Greek and Latin began paying off. I made a few friends and I secretly feared that I would go into advertising and I wrote letters to Winnie and I worried about her.

Then I read Exhibit J:

> The question "Why have there been no great women artists?" has led us to the conclusion, so far, that art is not a free, autonomous activity of a super-endowed individual, "influenced" by previous artists, and, more vaguely and superficially, by "social forces," but rather, that the total situation of art making, both in terms of the development of the art maker and in the nature and quality of the work of art itself, occur in a social situation, are integral elements of this social structure, and are mediated and determined by specific and definable social institutions, be they art academies, systems of patronage, mythologies of the divine creator, artist as he-man or social outcast.

The moment lived as it was being lived was not necessarily art but neither was it necessarily not art. I would have said I was not religious and I would have said I could be, and even was, a feminist, but at the same time I felt, and felt more, and felt more and more acutely, that I was not a free agent, was so determined by forces, was so fractional relative to the big puzzle of humanity, was not really anything.

> What is stressed in all these stories is the apparently miraculous, nondetermined, and asocial nature of artistic achievement; this semireligious conception of the artist's role is elevated to hagiography in the nineteenth century, when art historians, critics, and, not least, some of the artists themselves tended to elevate the making of art into a substitute religion, the last bulwark of higher values in a materialistic world.

A substitute religion. That rang big bells, the carillon bells that resounded in the atria of my finally fist-sized heart. I had to admit that I imagined art as a sacred antidote to the poison that had penetrated to my bone marrow, Minow's exhortations notwithstanding. The Gandhi-like non-violent passivism of my parents in spite of their saturation by TV, this, I tried to counterargue to myself, showed that the danger was

not so great. Yet, time and time again, I took off the shoes of the commercial world in which I walked willy-nilly, laid down my mat of maybe, and pointing to the East of Western Art, I rehearsed my belief that I, if not we, might be saved. It was just the bells of Harkness Tower reminding me to go back to my reading.

> The question "Why have there been no great women artists?" is simply the top tenth of an iceberg of misinterpretation and misconception; beneath lies a vast dark bulk of shaky idées reçues about the nature of art and its situational concomitants, about the nature of human abilities in general and of human excellence in particular, and the role that the social order plays in all of this.

I went so far as to take a Sociology course, though it was a bit like sitting in the omphalos of the bourgeois institution gazing into the omphalos of the bourgeois institution ad absurdum.

> To encourage a dispassionate, impersonal, sociological, and institutionally oriented approach would reveal the entire romantic, elitist, individual-glorifying, and monograph-producing substructure upon which the profession of

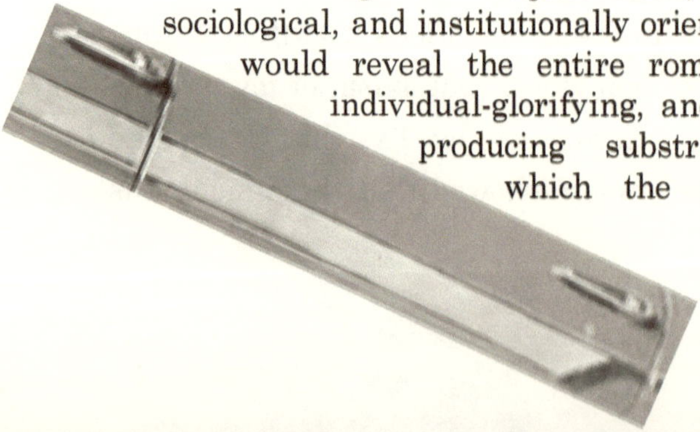

> art history is based, and which has only recently been called into question by a group of younger dissidents.

The following semester I looked for a class on dissidence. Luckily, there was one, in the Philosophy Department. I walked out of the seminar with friends but peeled off to go to the library while they peeled off to get high, to eat vegetarian foodstuffs, to play pinball, to rally outdoors, to proliferate Marxist-Leninist-Feminist cells indoors, to affirm affirmative action, and to imagine their wires tapped. I was an armchair sympathizer, investing in art futures, or rather future, my own. I was a Me generation ahead of my time. I noticed some cute girls, but my heart was not in it. Consciousness was the byword of college days, unconsciousness that of the nights. Winnie wrote to rib me: *Now you're studying to be an aesthetician?*

I wrote Winnie to say, *Om. Umbilicus novum.* Winnie wrote to say that she had met somebody, somebody military I supposed, and I supposed she thought she knew what she was doing. I said nothing because I knew nothing, and I didn't know what to say that was not anything.

> Behind the most sophisticated investigations of great artists — more specifically, the art-historical monograph, which accepts the notion of the great artist as primary, and the social and institutional structures within which he lived and worked as mere secondary "influences" or "background" — lurks the golden-nugget theory of genius and the free-enterprise conception of individual achievement. On this basis, women's lack of major achievement in art may be formulated as a syllogism: If women had the golden nugget of artistic genius then it would reveal itself. But it has never revealed itself. Q.E.D. Women do not have the golden nugget of artistic genius. If Giotto, the obscure shepherd boy, and van Gogh with his fits could make it, why not women?

Why not women? Winnie might have become someone who would prefer the enunciated muscles of a real man to what I had. Worse, she might not find my politics funny anymore. It might be like high school all over again, during which I lost her weekly, but never forever.

I could not know what I had in me; there was a pupal cast to the time outside the window. If Winnie could love someone else, I could too. Couldn't I. Choose something.

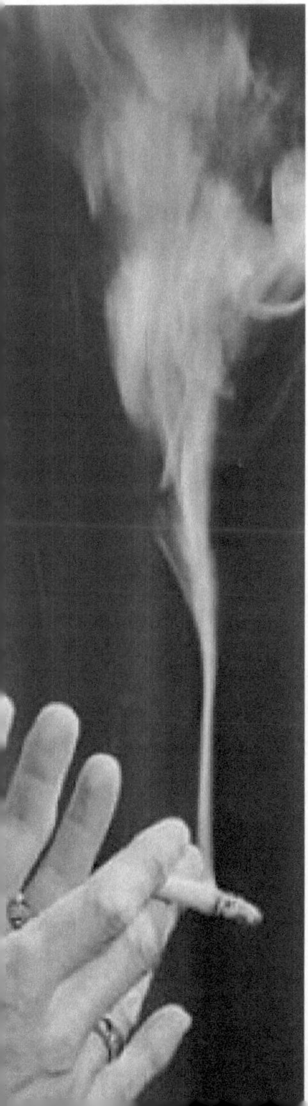

> Yet as soon as one leaves behind the world of fairy tale and self-fulfilling prophecy and, instead, casts a dispassionate eye on the actual situations in which important art production has existed, in the total range of its social and institutional structures throughout history, one finds

this from Winnie at the School of Killing Central America: *remember wearing wigs like in "Battle of Algiers"? — they showed us that film in Counterinsurgency to prepare us for a kind of war very different from the regular war we entered the Navy School for. They are preparing us for police missions against the civilian population, who have become our new enemy.*

I went home for the holidays and saw that "Candid Camera" had made a comeback. Mother and Dad roared along with canned laughter. In one episode, a vandal looked around to make sure he was unobserved before creating a piece he called "Pissed Off" by urinating on a Richard Serra — on a sculpture by him, that is. Oh no, that was an article in the paper. See, I saw that I should never have picked up the news again. I put it down. In "Mr. Vandal," the gang is stopping at an old town called McGrawsville when Quick Draw McGraw inherits it from his grandpappy. However, J. Wanton Vandal

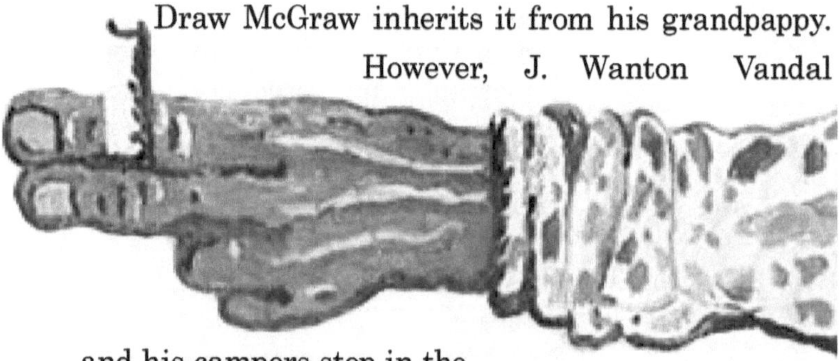

and his campers stop in the town and start demolishing antiques. It's up to Yogi and the gang to teach the kids the value of antique objects. Oh no, that was in the textbook lying open on the table, where Joseph Pierre Proudhon was quoted as saying that if "'the law of ideal and of capital' were subordinated to the workers' rights, there would be no iconoclasts or vandals anymore...." Tell it to the Marines. Or the CIA. Or the FCC.

Or God. A lot of J. Wanton Vandals have some sort of God driving them to the museum. While He idles in the No Standing zone, they do their thing, and are then apprehended on the spot, so God drives away again empty handed. Often, the J. Wantons want to be caught, sometimes to get some attention. In fact, many have wanted to go to jail because they want to get a free meal. I don't mean this like a Republican. I mean if the law of ideal and capital were subordinated to the workers' rights, there would be no iconoclasts or vandals any more. These ideas go back a long way, back before Marcel turned the first urinal upside down. For example, speaking of the tradition of chicks with blades and political statements to make, one Valentine Contrel, unemployed, naturally, offered Exhibit K as an explanation for why she attacked Ingres's *The Sistine Chapel* in the Louvre in 1907:

> It is a shame to see so much money invested in dead things like those at the Louvre collections when so many poor

devils like myself starve because they cannot find work. I have just spoiled a picture at the Louvre in order to be arrested. My name is Valentine Contrel, and I was born at Rouen in 1880. My parents died three years ago, leaving me penniless. I served as a governess in England, but English life did not suit me. I did dressmaking in Paris. I had to get up at four in the morning and work till midnight to earn 13 cents a day, and I could not pay my rent. I returned to my native town, but could earn my living no better there than in Paris. I came back to Paris and was determined to get "run in." The papers lately mentioned that a man had slashed a Louvre picture. That is what I must do to avenge myself. At 3 o'clock in the afternoon I went into the Louvre. As there was a crowd in all the galleries, I waited until 4:30 when the visitors began to leave, and went to the unfrequented Ingres room, where I chose the Sistine Chapel picture because it was not under glass. I had no intention of making a demonstration against religion. With a small pair of scissors I first tried to cut the Pope's eyes away, but the canvas was too thick, and I

had to content myself with slashing the figure and several others. I had to stop several times for fear of attracting the notice of the visitors. A young woman was copying near me, but she was too intent upon her work to notice me. When I thought I had done enough damage to be arrested, I went away and came here to give myself in charge. As a matter of fact, this is not the first outrage of this kind that I have committed. Some months ago, in a room of

> the Jardin des Plantes museum, I smashed a glass case containing a fine butterfly, which I destroyed. I was arrested, but the police let me go out of pity for the wretched penury I was in.

Being released was not, for Contrel, an opportunity to go get a job; it was an irony that couldn't go unpunished. Clearly some kind of contrarian, but one with a good point, Contrel didn't want a job; she wanted a permanent break: "I want to go to prison; I am tired of working. Wherever I go I have to be the servant of somebody or other. I want to eat and drink without working. I'll have myself sent to prison for life."

Ironically, in the same year of Contrel's outrage against *The Sistine Chapel* in Paris, over in Vienna, Sigmund Freud first published his "Obsessive Acts and Religious Practices" (although

he might have said there are no coincidences, that essay would only be reprinted in 1961). By 1907, Freud had probably forgotten about some trouble he had had with the help a few years earlier. But in 1901, he had had it with the butler who had pushed a dirty rag across a recently acquired canvas. Such things kept happening in his abode, injuries to his collectibles, as though with a will; it was uncanny. Or not: "When servants drop and break something fragile, our minds do not immediately fly to some psychological explanation, but once again, it is not unlikely that hidden motives are involved. Nothing is further from an uneducated person's mind than an appreciation of art and works of art. Unspoken hostility towards artistic items prevails among the servant classes, particularly when the objects, whose value they do not understand, give them extra work to do." If the servants suffer from class resentment, Doktor Freud, maybe it's because they've got to wipe your arts.

Mind aside, the mature brain processes information through transmission of axons at synapses. Once axons reach their targets, they form synapses, which permit electric signals in the axon to jump to the next cell, where they can either provoke or prevent generation of a new signal — kind of like what Jesse said. For processing to occur properly, the proper mechanisms must guide each axon to its proper target area. So let's talk about targets...like Klee's *The Fish* and paintings by Rubens and Lucas Cranach the Elder. In 1977, Hans-Joachim Bohlmann had worked his way through six cities, spraying sulfuric acid out of a disposable syringe at such works of art, until he was apprehended in Kassel on October 8. His diagnosis, the "tendency to accumulate aggression," had resulted in his being pensioned (nothing unconscious about it, contra Freud). But aggression didn't just accumulate in Bohlmann; he was compelled to relieve it through acts, like the bambinos with their Bobos (in spite of the punishment, *pace* Skinner). Aggression as capital, culture as battlefield. Bohlmann derived irresistible gratification from destroying objects that others loved and admired. So he attacked paintings. That's just psycho, however biochemical.

Maybe a vandal is always crazy, at least a little bit, at least for a little while, and very often he or she is a failed or frustrated artist. While they remain with the victimized work, waiting to be apprehended, they rehearse their statement of mission. Sometimes UFOs make him/her do it. Other times, he thinks the work is overrated. Often, she thinks she is acting as an artist. Sometimes they are doing it for Jesus. Occasionally, the vandal is a self-imagined agent of history, just helping along the inevitable. But lots of vandals simply don't like the work they attack.

It has always surprised me how often these vandals

react against art works they perceive as cold, but really, where's the surprise? The museums keep the stuff on ice. Like the one who kissed the Baer painting. Another version of this: in 1996, a J. Wanton Vandal, I mean an art student, ate blue cake icing and blue Jell-O in order to projectile vomit blue onto Piet Mondrian's *Composition in Red, White, and Blue* as it hung in

MoMA. "It was just so boring it needed some color," said Jubal Brown as he later vomited red on Raoul Dufy's *Harbour at le Havre* in the Art Gallery of Ontario. Or maybe he said it a few minutes later, after he wiped his mouth. "I found its lifelessness threatening and it made me sick." Sure, Mondrian with his rational lineation, the mystery of color reduced to liminal minimalia. Not my favorite either. But on the other hand, you might wonder why Mondrian's or Dufy's, or anyone else's, painting should have been other than lifeless, was any painting ever other than... lifeless....

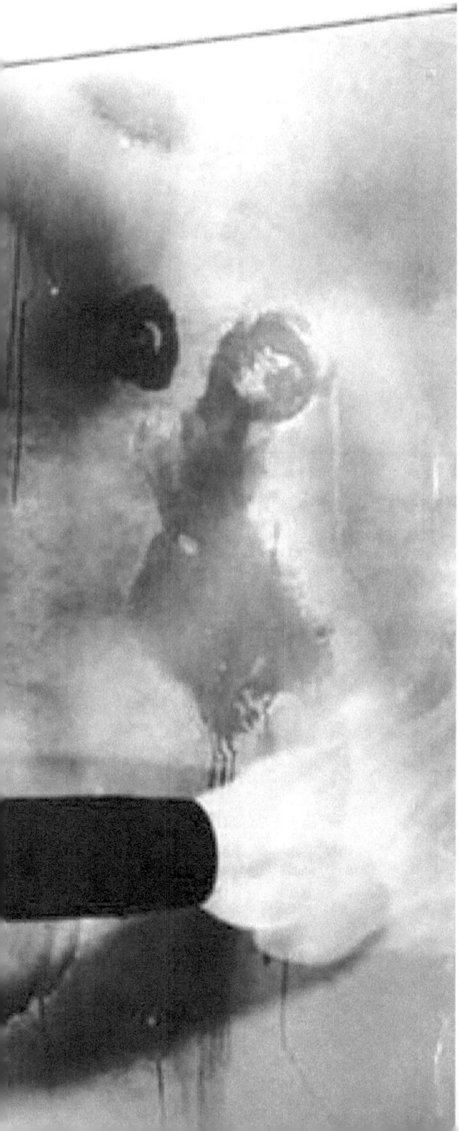

Winnie wrote to say, but no it couldn't have happened like that because how could she have written after she was already when the letter must have gone to Frank and Irene, no no, no letter could have gone to

Frank and Irene, and there would have been no letter for me, a phone call, there would have been there must have been the phone call of you are hearing the voice of a stranger say not only is this voice not the voice of the one most familiar to you but it is here to say you will never hear that most familiar voice again and in the infinity of time and the infinite slowness that sudden tragedy can pack into and draw out of one minute, then two, then five minutes you will realize that that is not the voice of a stranger, it is Winnie herself, but no again and forever, in the split second that never ends, it is finally not Winnie, it is Irene.

The sound of not-Winnie, there will never be Winnie, that sound burned into the burning new grooves into the remember the synapses you formed in tandem with the one who is no longer the other one of you. The sound I will hear forever in the absence of the sound of Winnie, someone suddenly a stranger, Irene, suddenly, strangely, saying "I have some hard news." Already everything was all wrong. Already it had been since she was a toddler, shooting. Would we recover? What if Sartre was right? *Yes,* he wrote in the Preface to Fanon's *The Wretched of the Earth, Violence, like Achilles' spear, can heal the wounds it has inflicted.*

Right in the goddam middle of college, on some fucking "exercise" of the kind no government will ever explain, even to its own most bereft, Winnie died. Do you think I lost my mind then? No. I was shell-shocked at first. And I was torn up for years — way beyond sad — and angry. Betrayed, confused, desolate, A to Z of pain and back again to A, sometimes obsessed, and then again I would forget Winnie had died, though I never forgot that she had lived. I felt naked, in a way, uncovered, unprotected, alone, misunderstood by anyone who was not Winnie and absolutely permanently shellacked into the failure to communicate that had always been our m.o. anyway, hers and mine, even though it had felt like fate that we would go toe-to-toe from the blanket to the grave, like Roger Maris and Mickey Mantle in the "home run derby" in our eternal first summer. I could go on and on. I did, in fact, at her funeral.

Although, or perhaps because, it was completely inappropriate, at Winnie's service, I read from Sartre on Fanon, published in 1961, Exhibit L:

> . . . in a time of helplessness, murderous rampage is the collective unconscious of the colonized.

A somebody military shot daggers at me, Frank and

Irene were perplexed, and the coffin was fake. So I went on:

> Terrified, yes. At this new stage colonial aggression is internalized by the colonized as a form of terror. By that I mean not only the fear they feel when faced with our limitless means of repression, but also the fear that their own fury inspires in them. They are trapped between our guns, which are pointing at them, and those frightening instincts, those murderous impulses, that emerge from the bottom of their hearts and that they don't always recognize. For it is not first of all their violence, it is ours, on the rebound, that grows and tears them apart; and the first reaction by these oppressed people is to repress this shameful anger that is morally condemned by them and us, but that is the only refuge they have left of their humanity.

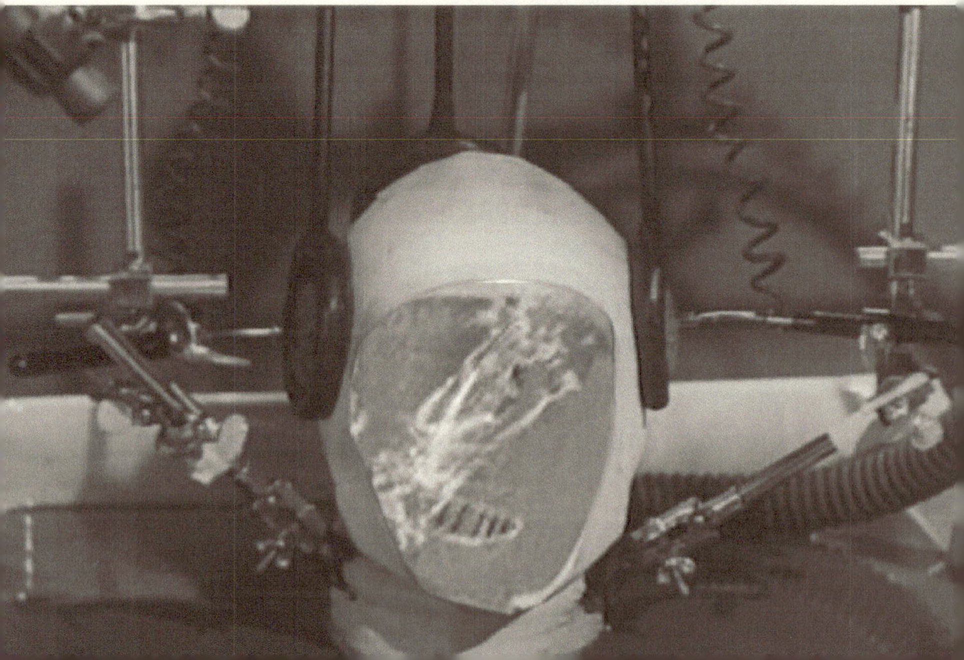

It is so difficult to have no one to blame, I said. No one but us chickens. Look in the mirror and see the whites of our eyes. Can we get the words "friendly fire," or the taste of its ash, out of our mouths? Can we locate the enemy outside of our bodies, ourselves, when that enemy is coursing through our blood? Meaning to shoot at Him, we shoot our own selves in the feet. Or the heart, as the case may be. I like to think protocol might change as a result of this, that Winnie's death might not be for naught, that we might now beat our swords into ploughshares, "But you can't; there is no way out." I like to think Winnie's death, like her life, is unique, but I am one naive fuck. But but but.

> But in actuality, as we all know, things as they are and as they have been, in the arts as in a hundred other areas, are stultifying, oppressive, and discouraging to all those, women among them, who did not have the good fortune to be born white, preferably middle class and, above all, male. The fault lies not in our stars, our hormones, our menstrual cycles, or our empty internal spaces, but in our institutions and our education — education understood to include everything that happens to us from the moment we enter this world of meaningful symbols, signs, and signals.

Your Honor, I was as lucid as I have ever been. Hopeless, but lucid. I explained that I studied art before finally alienating the entire assembly. In a proper eulogy, there must be the bittersweet anecdote, so I told them about how Winnie mistook the nude for the naked, but that it boiled, bombed and burned down to the same thing:

> First of all, we must confront an unexpected sight: the striptease of our humanism. Not a pretty sight in its nakedness: nothing but a dishonest ideology, an exquisite justification for plundering; its tokens of sympathy and affection, alibis for our acts of aggression. Not without excellent results in the shape of palaces, cathedrals, and centers of industry....

I heard murmurs. My parents would not meet my gaze. Frank and Irene's grief must have been momentarily suspended in their stupefaction, and in their regret that they had asked me to speak, though they would never thank me for that, and soon the regret reached back to comprehend a moment in the Boston Lying-In Hospital.

> Come now! If you are not a victim when the government you voted for and the army your young brothers served in, commits "genocide," without hesitation or remorse, then, you are undoubtedly a torturer.

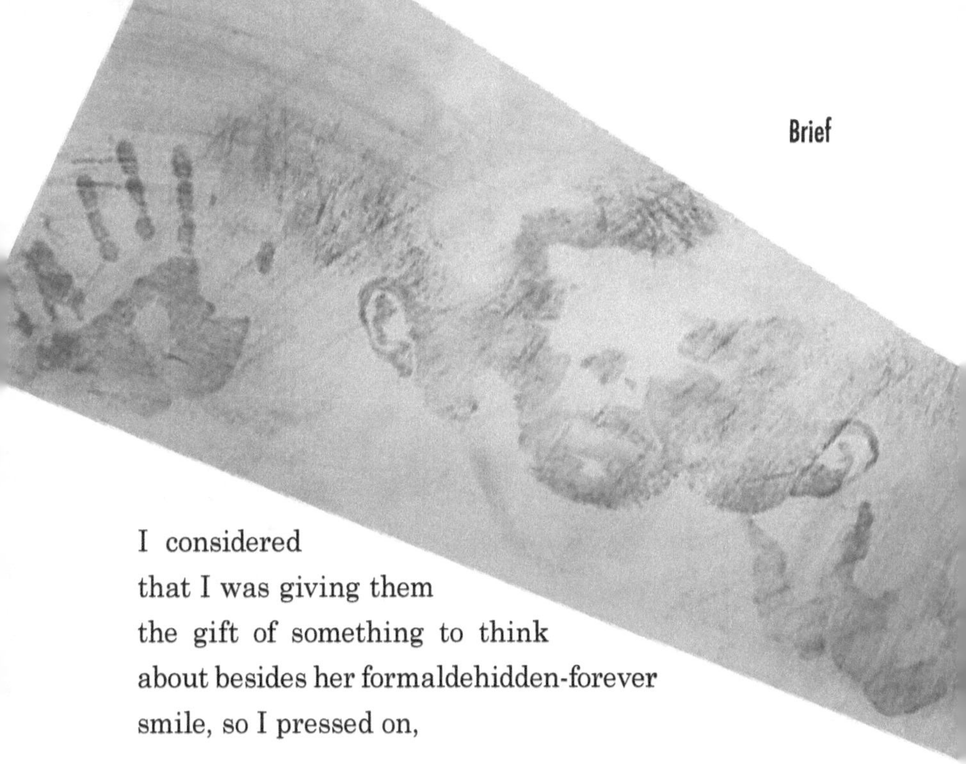

I considered
that I was giving them
the gift of something to think
about besides her formaldehidden-forever
smile, so I pressed on,

> You know full well we are exploiters.... What empty chatter: liberty, equality, fraternity, love, honor, country, and what else? This did not prevent us from making racist remarks at the same time: dirty nigger, filthy Jew, dirty Arab. Noble minds, liberal and sympathetic...claimed to be shocked by the inconsistency, since the only way the European could make himself man was by fabricating slaves and monsters.

I beg your pardon for this Riff, but as he says to Tony in *West Side Story*, and spoke on film the year Winnie and I emerged, birth to earth, 1961, from womb to tomb, that is how long I have known Winnie. And now she's just another Anybodys in the graveyard of "country." I do not beg the pardon of the United States of America. No, I curse *the name of a country; be careful lest it become the name of a neurosis in **1961**.*

I tried to find a redemptive note to end on even as I was borne back ceaselessly to the beginning. So wretched was I, and so stuck in *The Wretched of the Earth* to which Winnie would return a half-hour later, this was the best I could do:

Frank and Irene have not spoken to me since, which strains certain social occasions for my parents. That's life.

Have I ever fallen in love? With anyone else? I looked around at my classmates. "We were born the

year Life cereal hit the market — how do I know you're for real?" she said as she pulled the pin from the grenade.

"We were born the year Silly Putty went international and I should take you seriously?" she said as she snapped the top off the can, becoming a hit in the Soviet Union, Germany, Italy, Netherlands, and Switzerland.

"We were born the year the first alien abduction was reported, how could I believe anything you say?"

And on and on. I couldn't hack it. All the Reclina-rocker jokes. All the dress code jokes, and the student handbook lying open forbade women to wear slacks or Bermuda shorts to class, dinner, or in public living rooms, and required men to wear a long coat, even when "merely crossing campus to attend a function where slacks or Bermuda shorts are the appropriate dress."

I left school and I wandered the world, which luckily looked typical enough. From the Falkland Islands to Bhopal, I wondered about the map; if $x=R\lambda$ and $y=2R\sin\phi$ (which is Esperanto for the Gall-Peters projection), then Managua and Tehran are adjacent. Through the hole in the ozone layer, I pondered the big round installation in the sky, our sick shit planet. Earth. I spent years looking at the petroglyphs and pillars of the Ajanta caves, ziggurats and tapestries,

Faience and little figurines like the Venus of Tan-tan and the big-ass Buddhas of Bamiyan. Those days you could do that kind of thing on five dollars a day. Or given inflation, seven. When I ground to a halt, it turned out that I had grown up. I was ready to complete my education and get to work.

It.is.said: in the young primate cerebral cortex, the connections between neurons are greater in number and twice as dense as those in an adult primate. Connections that are active and generating electrical currents survive, whereas those with little or no activity are lost. Thus, the circuits of the adult brain are formed, at least in part, by sculpting away inactive connections. It. is. thus. that. we. slow. down. By sculpting away. The. metaphors. phor. brain activity. include. cellular. suicide. wiring. paring back. pruning. sculpting. As if I coulda been canning tomatoes. If

I only had a heart. But no. I had to. Do what I did. I.conoclasm. I.nqui. I couldna done otherwise. Duh.

My travels had restored my faith in art. And. cemented. My despair in a public sphere. Where words still carried the day. It was only when I got home that I lost my tread. Maybe it was precisely when I turned the TV back on and saw another war brewing in the Middle East, which could really have been just about anytime in the last several decades, but now TVs got piled on top of each other making art art, which really topped op art: now, we could see scuds at night piled on top of each other as art art. I had been to the real Baghdad, but on the screen, Baghdad was green. I turned off the TV almost immediately, but it was too late. Where could I turn to tune in the colors of my own immediate agency? Nowhere. But.

My diminishing brain plasticity, my adolescent, and

my less-dramatic adult, development, these have had disturbingly pacifying, nay, narcotizing, effects; smoke damage to one's own luxuries blocks out the pathos of the hurricane, the earthquake, the child soldier selling his little sister, or I have less time to read the paper, or times still are a-changing, and nowadays people are less determined by historical events. Maybe I'm wrong about everything, and individual personality and action bear no trace of history, and history itself is nothing more than a fractally complex series of accidents. Like the one in which Steve Wynn put his right elbow through Picasso's *Le Rêve*. "Oh shit, look what I've done," he said. Winnie would have roared. Wynn's *retinitis pigmentosa* affected his peripheral vision, and by extension his proprioceptive judgment. So, in a way, as he stood in front of the painting — worth $139 million dollars — Wynn's focus on his friends — Nora Ephron, Nicholas Pileggi, and Barbara Walters — as they stood around admiring it with him, may have endangered the painting. (Or, depending how you look at it, Wynn may have breathed fresh air into the painting.) Luckily, he owned *Le Rêve*. Luckily, it had appreciated $80.6 million dollars since he had acquired it less than ten years earlier. In the time that Ephron, and Pileggi, and Walters spent staring at Wynn instead of the painting, it appreciated another

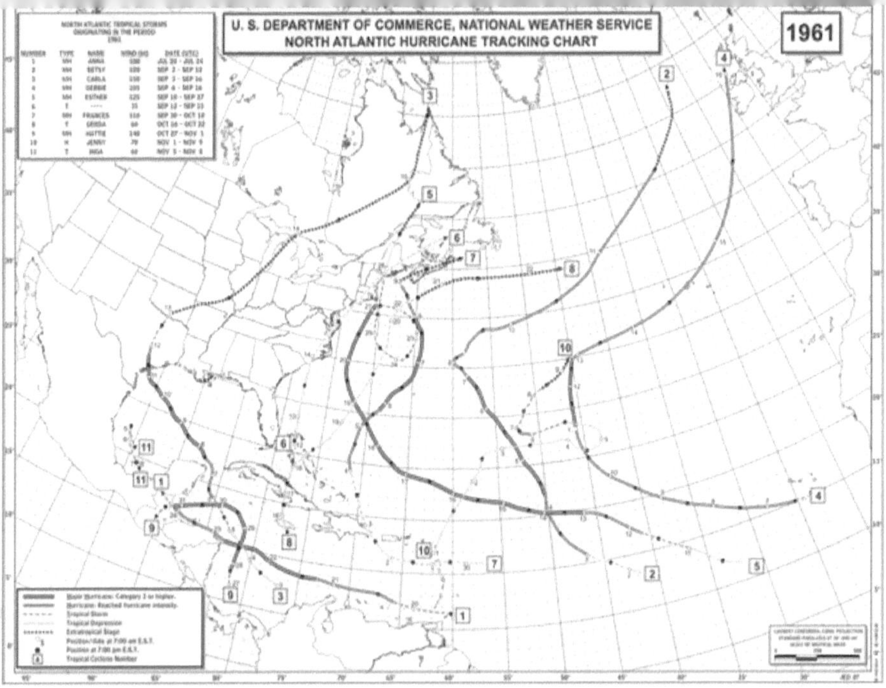

176 dollars. I appreciated the gesture myself, but it doesn't count because it was unintentional.

I'm not joking. I mean, not like some joker walks into a bar says "That photograph always bugged the hell out of me," pulls a sawed-off shotgun from his coat pocket, fires on a Richard Avedon, and sends bullets through two women attending a Daughters of the American Revolution convention. That's not funny; someone could have gotten hurt. And another sawed-off shotgun came out from under another overcoat, this one belonging to an ex-soldier in London, who went from museum to museum looking for a place to commit his act of vandalism. He settled on Leonardo's *The Virgin and the Child* at the National Gallery and plugged Saint Anne and John

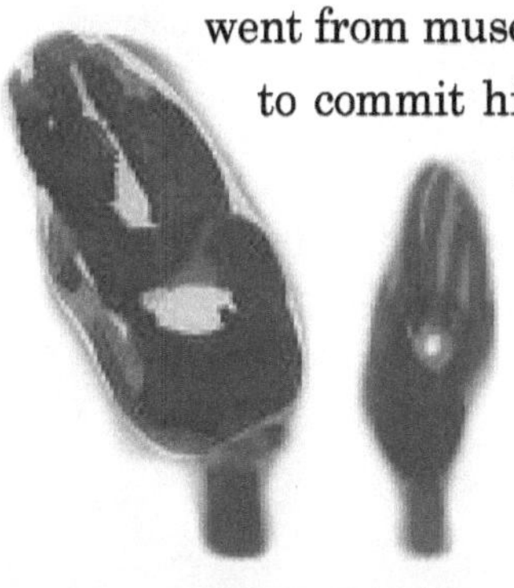

the Baptist. Afterwards, Robert Arthur Cambridge explained that "the relevance in my action can be seen in the comparison between the great achievements of mankind contained in the National Gallery, and the scene of degradation and decay as witnessed under the railway arches at Charing Cross." That *is* serious, but so are firearms, too serious, and they landed him in a high-security hospital for testing. Cambridge may be right, but his line belongs in a book, or an article, or a pamphlet, along with this artifact, authored by a Son of the French Revolution: "In the name of the Sovereignty of the people...we strike with death this abode of crime whose royal magnificence was an insult to the poverty of the people...toys...and spoils of prejudice and arrogance." Righteous, no doubt (if a little bit Frenchish), along the lines of Valentine Contrel, but there's no excuse for guns, and frankly, this line is truly outmoded.

Your Honor, everything I have done has been for the present, in the hope that it will forever remain in the present. Rauschenberg erased a De Kooning, with the blessing of the latter. Picasso painted over a Modigliani. Pastiche is just PoMo for pentimento. Picasso himself said, "Ultimately, what is important about a picture is the legend it has created, not whether it is preserved or not." Art lives many lives and must not be allowed to die while its message is ever more urgent. Guns, knives, broken bottles, and refurbished grenades are one thing, but I would not traffic in those found objects, and like it or not, today's urgent art of the people is writing. All over, again. I could, willfully, breathe new life into a painting that screamed for peace while patrons milled about whispering. Or so I told myself...in a moment of temporary insanity.

In that moment, I went to work in the midtown temple of Modern Art. I wore the requisite overcoat and cited the handbag. I was all dolled up with the performativity of the trade, lipstick and acid in the bag, bladder full, and a belly full of Jell-O. But the tool of art, the article of war, the articulate instrument, would be the painted word. I wanted to bring the art absolutely up to date, to retrieve it from art history and give it life. I wanted to dwell within the act of the painting's creation, get involved with the making of the work, put my hand within it and by that act encourage the individual viewer to challenge it, deal with it and thus see it in its dynamic raw state as it was being made, not as a piece of history. So it was *with* the artist, I wrote, actually spray-painted, in big bright red letters, in a copy-cat crime of appreciation and appropriation of, an homage to Tony Shafrazi, when he tagged Picasso's anti-war masterpiece with "KILL LIES ALL." A class on a fieldtrip from Scarsdale High watched. I told them I was an artist, but they looked stunned; they couldn't move. I guess I didn't have to curse like that in front of a bunch of teenagers. But I told the police too, down at the station house on 54th, "I'm an artist and I wanted to tell the truth." What did I mean? Let the critics figure it out; that's not my job. "Criminal mischief" — that was my job, in that moment. We're all familiar with the charges; I just want to say it was a temporary post, and I have already vacated it.

Or as one Mark Bridger put it, "I was in a carpe diem frame of mind; tomorrow may not be available." Bridger was the penniless artist who poured black ink into Damien Hirst's white lamb floating in a tank of formaldehyde, *Away from the Flock*. Bridger too meant to work *with*, not against the artist: "To live is to do things, I was providing an interesting addendum to his work. In terms of conceptual art, the sheep had already made its statement. Art is there for creation of awareness and I added to whatever it was meant to say." There's always something for critics to do, though artists like Bridger go unemployed. As for Hirst, whose sheep

made him a bundle, when the prosecutor asked him why he was an artist, Hirst said, "I don't know. I've always been an artist." I defy you to tell me that Hirst makes more sense than Bridger, though the former made more money, and the latter was found guilty of criminal damage, fined for compensation — it cost 1,000 pounds to remove the pigment — and released from payment on the grounds of insufficient means. In defense of one or both of them, it's not hard to imagine Hirst and Bridger at the same conceptual table, where the restorers break bread with the critics, tossing meanings in the mixed salad of the museum cafe, with the dressing of the times, better for the arteries than Mother's old recipes.

As for my own defense, consider this: mental incompetence kept one Bobby Frank Cherry out of court, while his old KKK buddy the *compos mentis* Thomas Blanton, Jr. got tried, decades after the fact, for bombing the Sixteenth Street Baptist Church in Birmingham in 1963, and killing 11-year-old Denise McNair and 14-year-olds Addie Mae Collins, Cynthia Wesley, and Carole Robertson. The boys at the Bureau bugged his apartment, and thus could offer prosecutors proof of Tommy Blanton, Jr. at the age of 24 saying he was through with women and would "stick to bombing churches." (This, while

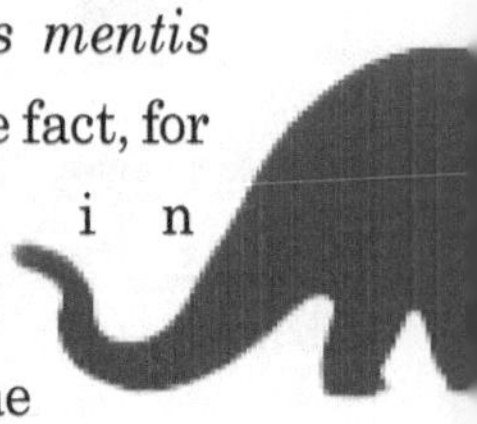

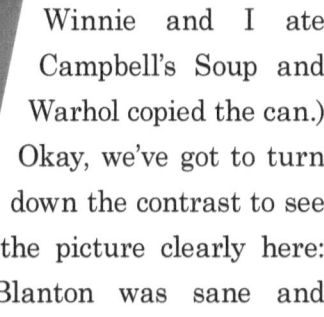

Winnie and I ate Campbell's Soup and Warhol copied the can.) Okay, we've got to turn down the contrast to see the picture clearly here: Blanton was sane and went free for 37 years before coming to trial, the FBI was the good guy, and Cherry never got tried. Total scambigram. Impossible though it may be, it's important to try to figure out what is insane and what is its opposite, like a little judicial D.E.S., try to prevent a miscarriage of justice here.

So. If it's not too late, Your Honor, I will show you that such a thing as temporary insanity exists. Watch this exhibit: I just have to think back, back and forth and back. Follow the bouncing ball. Sing along with me, back through the history of the present to 1961, the year the historians in the Office of the Historians in the Bureau of Public Affairs started tracking "Significant Terrorist Incidents." Your Honor, may I ask you how old you are? And how old are *you*? And *you*? And *you*? And can I get a witness? Or can I get a little Sympathy for the Imp of the Perverse Blowin' in the Winds of Change Burning Down the House. The ticky-tacky stuff you're soaking in, call it

ideology, call it hegemony, call it the Situation Normal All Fucked Upside same rightside up as down, it looks like 1961 no matter how you slice it looks like the best thing since mother's milk. January 30, that day of days, Your Honor, the FBI terminated New Criticism, and after that, after such vandellas, what forgiveness, thanks for the memories, for after all what's left of the Left now that The Vandellas have taken the handles. After Vandella, pleased to meet you hope you guess how to look at a pick-axe handle the same way twice the price of the

protest against the marketing of art which naturally or divinely transcends mortal accounting, in art no different from the way Frank and Irene do it up in Massachusetts feet shifting in their shoes on Route 1 on the North Shore of where Nixon lied as he did on Route 66 and on the other Route 1, the 1 running right through a hole in San Luis Obispo, green canvas

of the Pacific Ocean where sea lions and baby seals protest the environmental pollution my good mother my good father wrought with nothing in them but what you would call love, shiver, slip an' slide, as they did in the slime of their times, my mother and father hoping for nothing but better for me than this but there is nothing better Mother, Dad, nothing better than the miasma of opportunity out of which the writer draws a picture of how this will fly amid UFOs and hammers fleshing out the insolvency and the downright degradation of the dried paint and layers upon layers of everything false. but *le non-dit*. I'm talking about *LE NON-DIT.* So sue me motherfucker up against the wall, from get down to up against the glass ceiling with the static electricity soft against the little hairs on your cheek as you hug — the TV — while art in the hands of the few withheld from the many is what makes you so great

— yet the FBI says you are not so great — the FBI hides the files that reveal the real rebozo, the original vandella, the original J. Wanton, won't you guess his name. It's Cortés whose ship I passed like a ship in the night of the centuries later still his pathways etched in the very wavy water and in the junkyard of satellites we used to call the sky when we think about the way we remember him Navy SEALing wax *avant la lettre*, and see now the way we iterate his *non-dit* name right here in court, his name emblazoned on the cortex of the veal farm, the chain-linked stories of the Mexican border, the mall, the overly Euclidean grid of the cities

where graffiti smushiti scratchiti and the *vox pentimento* you think inside the box of I scream you scream we all scream in the subways and on the billboards reliving the very cemented edifices of sentimentation built on the bloody sand of if we had come in peace don't you think things would have gone a lot differently. Reliving and relieving ourselves in the process in the pissing contest that never ends in and on and as the arts. Cortés, get in line for the lineup, get your paranoid polaroid portraiture AKA mug shot right here, are you guilty of dots of color, are you reponsible for all that lousy-with-cops weather and the thermodynamics of irreversible processes, I. Prirogine, I, Inqui, I want to know. Cortés, don't change your ad campaign — even over decades. Do I contradict myself? Doing so will destroy penetration. Surely, Cortés, you will agree with charges of perversion and entrapment, on top of obscenity, and of underdogging up the Rocky Mountain Bullwinkle doohickey of your exploratory surgery on the frontal lobe of the people who would bake their bricks in the sun if if if you had only come in peace rather than paving the way for this: In Colombia recently, at the same time that a bloody assault was underway in Medellín, a statue by Fernando Botero representing a dove and entitled *The Bird* was blown up, probably by drug dealers objecting to the symbol of peace and to the sculptor's

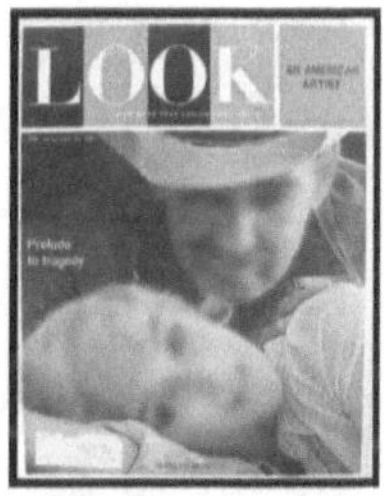

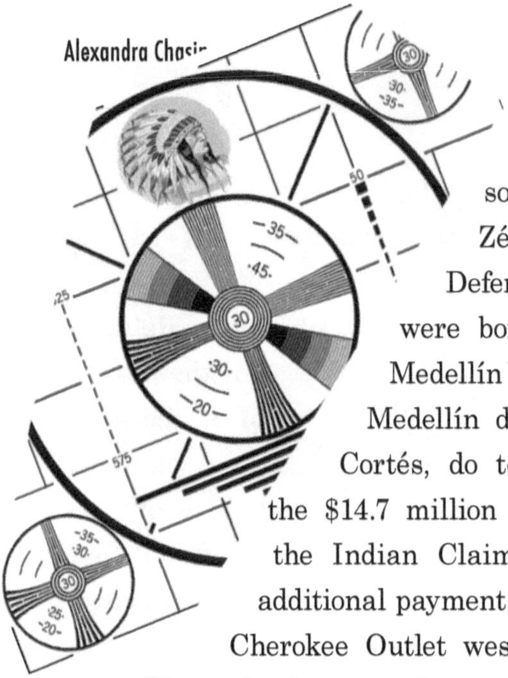

son, Fernando Botero Zéa, the Minister of Defense. Cortés, you were born in the original Medellín but to the derviative Medellín do you now return. Cortés, do token gestures like the $14.7 million award in 1961 by the Indian Claims Commission for additional payment for land in the Old Cherokee Outlet west of the Arkansas River, do they quench even one of the thirsty flames consuming your immortal soul from 1547 until now and then and again and still and all consuming until 1961 comes a second time? I will — I will hold the two hands of swearing an oath in the air to claim — responsibility — to claim I can do better I swear I will do better, Your Honor, whereas art is a luxury whereas intent to preserve whereas the origin of species like you adapt to the siren call of get your daily shock of the new right here while The Old Way whispers: *lifeless... Algerian... miniature... symbolic violence.* The Old Way whispers: *Penetration*: The percentage of people who remember your current advertising. *Usage Pull*: The percentage among people who remember versus don't remember your advertising. The Old Way whispers:

Rembrandt continues to grow as a company and in the whitening category to provide our customers with the best product in the market. Intense Stain. Peroxide. Doubling the effectiveness effectively doubles the flavor, doubles the doubles the unsaid species under which we labor because it goes without saying. Pardon my acid refluxus repeating on me. Carpe that. I'll stop right here; let me just pull up to the bumper of a golden age of poetry and power of which this noonday's the beginning hour. In the august occasions of the state, Today is for my cause a day of days.

Look around you, what do you see—

— oh god. What did I — I did this? I made this unholy mess? Well,
doesn't

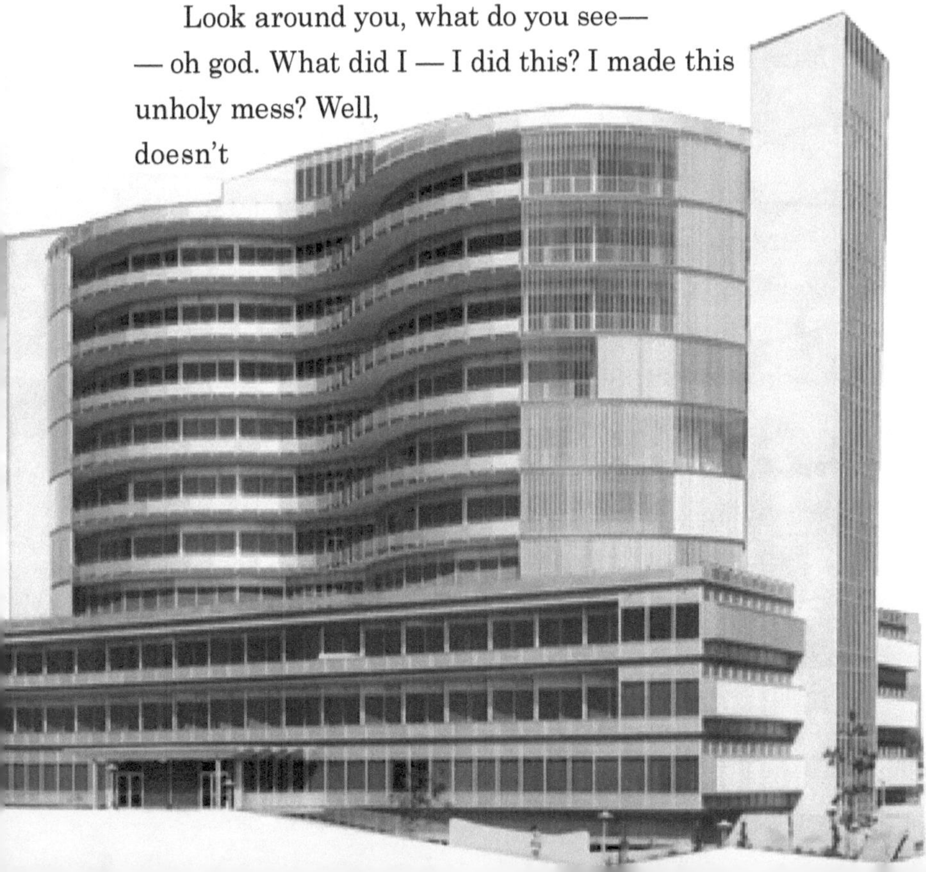

that just prove my point? The state I was in. Those things didn't have any evidentiary status anyway, and shouldn't have had, not since a little loop of wire and a cardboard butterfly were found among Walt Whitman's personal effects after his death. When he was still alive, he had attached himself to those effects and had a photograph taken to prove that he "had the knack for attracting birds and butterflies and other wild critters." The wire and the fraudulent symbol of eternal life — dead like him, the imaginary birds, the fake butterfly, and these shredded images too, just as dead except perhaps for their brief moment in flight, all of them pointing, as they flutter about, to my determining influences, hereby reduced to chaotic contingencies, not unlike the effect that cardboard butterfly would have had if it could have flapped its wings. In China. In 1961. So many contingent determinants unfolding... upside...down. Let them fall where they may.

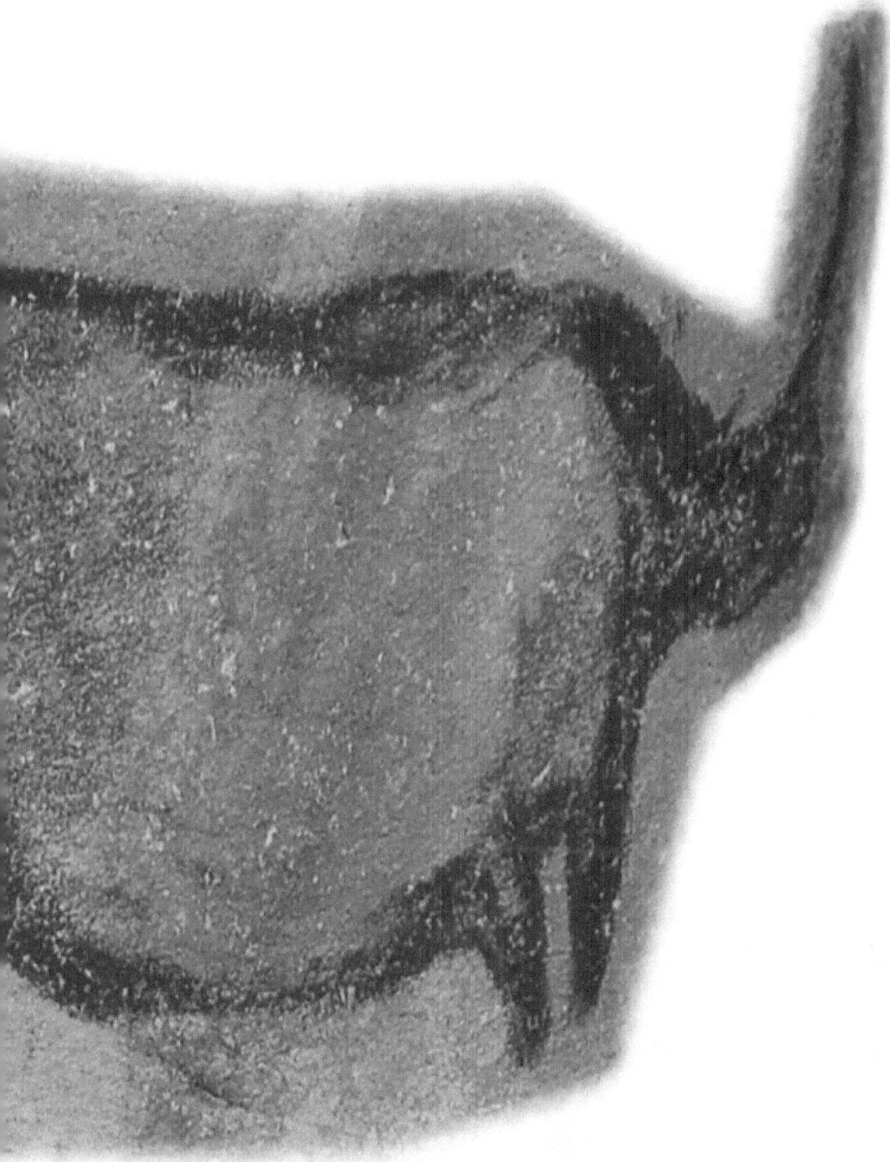

Their admissibility would have been at your discretion anyway, Your Honor, and you might have questioned the authenticity and you would certainly have doubted the relevance (you'd say I shredded that concept early on), and you may well have restated the opinion of your forebear, pronouncing in Cunningham v. Fair Haven & Westville R. Co. in 1899:

> It is common knowledge that as to such matters, either through want of skill on the part of the artist, or inadequate instruments or materials, or through intentional and skillful manipulation, a ---------- may not only be inaccurate but dangerously misleading.

On the other hand, even paintings — without the realness claims of photography to which Walt Whitman gave the lie when photography was in its infancy — have sometimes been used as legal evidence, as with the

work of David Olère, the Holocaust survivor whose paintings of Auschwitz testified to the realness of the gas chambers, and who could quibble with that. You see, I came prepared with the tools of your trade too.

So authentication and relevance are relative. Relatively meaningless. Meaning, only, with all due

respect, maybe pictures are effectively and forever without meaning, and art history is the bruise that has grown up around that injury. If we stab the canvas, if we tear up our icons, no less than if we worship them, we only hurt ourselves. And nothing brings Walt or Winnie back to life — not me, not art, not General Electric — or peace to Earth. The bruise on Steve Wynn's elbow testifies to the force of pure reflex, so much of which is educated out of us — not counting the autonomic functions of the heart. I must have forgotten where I am…in history. Now, and here, where there's no original — in print, in paint, in pixel, or person — and copies of any generation are closer to the thing copied than any duplicate ever was. What remains of the differences between Winnie and me? Not counting the autonomic functions of the heart. Excuse me, I lost my lossy compression for a moment, but I'm okay now.

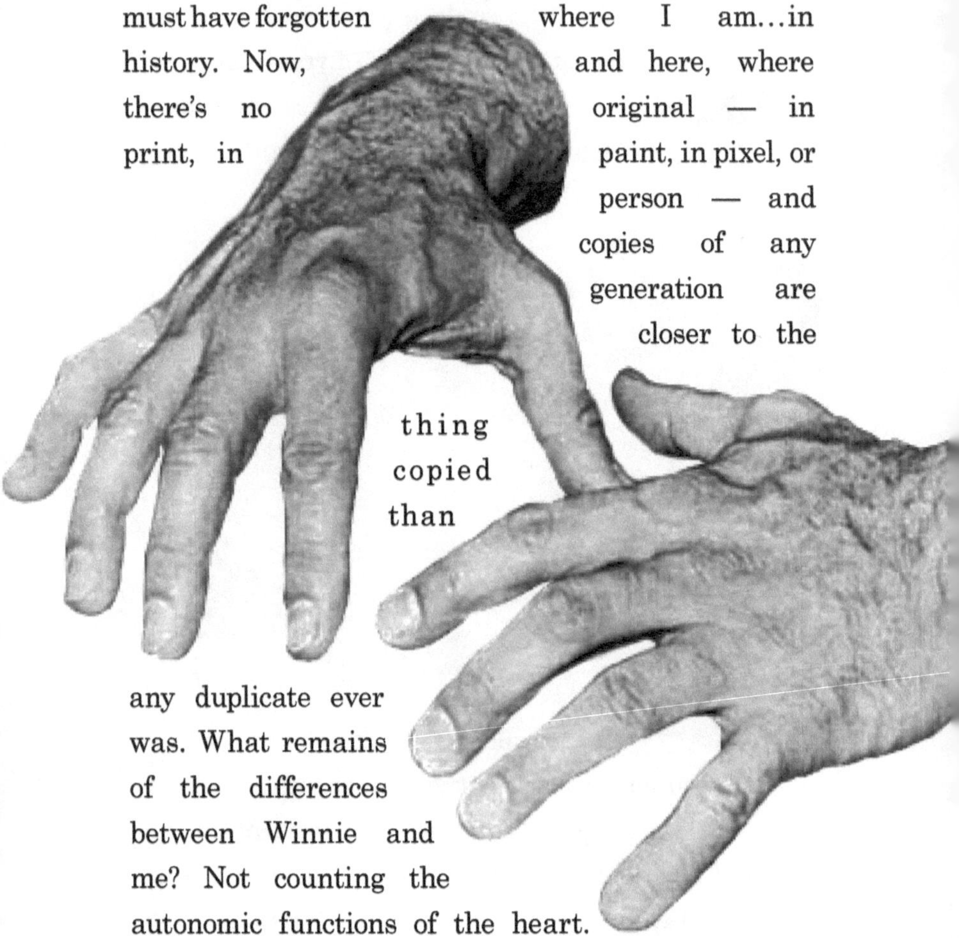

Your Honor, in the old days there was an academy

of art—and its twinship with a fine tradition of refuseniks—some slice of pretension to social good — but now—my parents may they retire in peace in venues known to the well endowed in the large city under which we seal Your Honor, trust me and dollars, we'll do the right thing. I will build a space, a collection, a temple, a gesture to genius, a true contribution to society.

I was just trying to accelerate the inevitable tendency of the dialectic of art production in a late capitalist context. Those who do not stand in the river of history swim in it.

No sir, I'm not any more or less cynical than I ever was. Differently so. Now I understand....

Now. And then I will write an article and publish it like a regular jerk, posing questions like, *How long does the work of art endure? Can we speak of the use/ misuse of the theory of it? Could it be said that all objects die — spectacles more spectacularly — symbols more symbolically*? I will play in my pen with my peer-reviewed puns. I will trot out ever-tamer notions in the appropriate pages, reviewing, first, the literature on symbolic violence, aggression, the judgment in play. I will pose, like a legitimated poseur: *Why vandalize art objects rather than other objects, like women?*

Your Honor, expert testimony will distinguish me from the Rockefellers, who destroyed a mural by Diego

Rivera and never got busted, and Richard Nixon, who said: "There is a need to investigate 'objectionable art' in governmental buildings with the view to obtaining removal of all that is found to be inconsistent with American ideals and principles," on the slippery slope to the really criminally insane, like the Taliban, who destroyed those big Buddhas, and the Huns. Yes, art is to be feared, yes, but capital and the state can now walk hand in hand without fear of it. This is the moment. Now that...an expert reads Exhibit N from a book, not his own:

> Many of today's art attackers, like the *Nude in the Mirror* slasher, are more vandals than iconoclasts. True iconoclasts seek to weaken religious or political institutions by attacking the dogmas and conventions central to the institution's authority. This is why Byzantine Emperor Leo III ordered all icons of Jesus, the Virgin Mary, and the saints destroyed in the 8th century, or why John Calvin, a leader of the Protestant Reformation, supported the removal of Catholic art in existing churches to be adapted for Protestant worship. Rather than opposing any particular policy or action, iconoclasts, in the true sense of the word, resist the entire institution itself.

Does that sound like me? Sure, I'm a pain in the ass, but I'm small potatoes. Small potatoes and sane tomatoes. There's only one institution I stand here to resist today. For a lark, I refused to sign the self-control contract there, not realizing that way would lead to one of the padded cells. Showerhead so close to the wall I can't hang myself. Mirror not a mirror, more aluminumy than glass, not glass at all, so I can't break it and cut myself. No towel racks, guess why. Plasticated shatter-proof windows don't open so I can't escape, in case I'm thinking if I could just get out the window and off the grounds and hitch a ride into town, I could kill myself. Talk about wackadoodle.

As to the crazies, who knows who those are. Those who can't adjust their personal screen. Me, if I can't escape the monetarization of art — if I can't lick 'em, or kiss 'em, or piss on 'em, or vomit on 'em — I can at least join 'em. The arts. The artists. The damned patrons. If I get out of this with nothing more than a phat fine, I'll set out straightaway to get the backing I need, and pull the past out of the toilet, the dustbin, the has-been, this bin, and that bin. It might be the first time in history an artist is proved to be sane. But Freud didn't get me into this and Freud won't get me out; he's busy trying to pick up the pieces of his broken little figurines.

So where does that leave us, Your Honor? With an eternal inability, collective and individual, to time

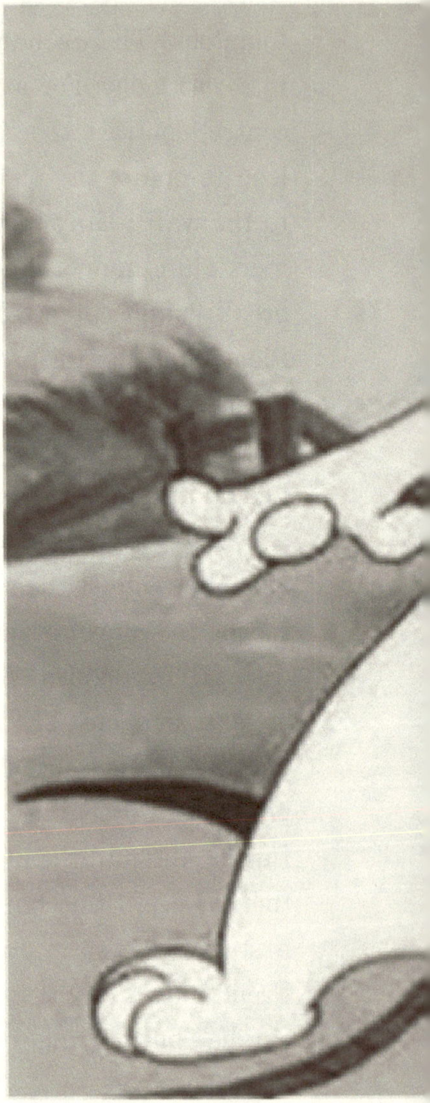

out vertically, to live on the longitudes of past, present, and future, to resign ourselves to historical contingency and bad motives, to know why we go to war the same way any single latitude wends its way around the globe — seamless and imaginary — no hint of where it began or whether it will ever leave off, as it rounds mountains and keeps ending up back where it started when it never really moved an inch. Because that way of drawing the world is just a choice among choices, neither bad nor good nor really, originally, ours. But it's got a mighty grip on those of us who ever believed everything they ever heard and saw. Unmolested by satellite dish, unlike me, lies that line of latitude, which has always already caught its own tail. That lie works for us, works its way back before our other meanings

of line. We can't go on but we do go on. Yes, yes Your Honor, I have gone on. Was I crazy? Am I still? We

there ar

Alexandra Chasin

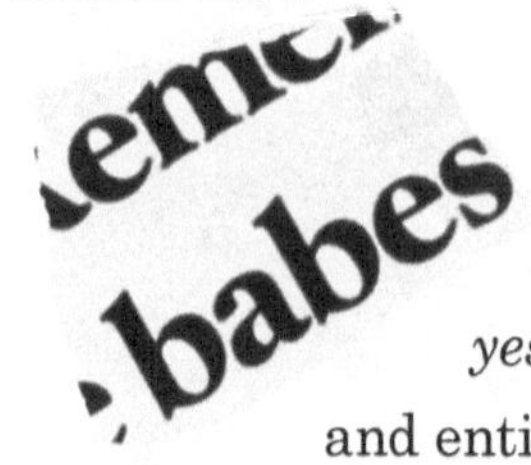

will, we have, come as close to *yes, temporarily*, as a subsequent and entirely credible *no* will allow.

Your Honor, picture this: there's a gallery midtown with my name on it, purveying fine works of graffiti, the occasional Basquiat, the not-unheard-of Keith Haring. There are three homes — a loft in Soho, a house in the Hamptons, and a flat in Paris — décor-ed to the hilt. All that is missing is a woman who died as a girl. I preview for you tomorrow and tomorrow and tomorrow: stemware and pressed dress suits, clients who like the hit of the third-rail, and will pay a little extra for the badass aura. All that's left to cover is today. It had to happen — that I would emerge all Yankee Doodle Dandy from the latter half of the 20th century, entrepreneurial, that is, and that art would imitate a longitude or a latitude for that matter, come full circle. Not because closure demands it — closure is dead. I

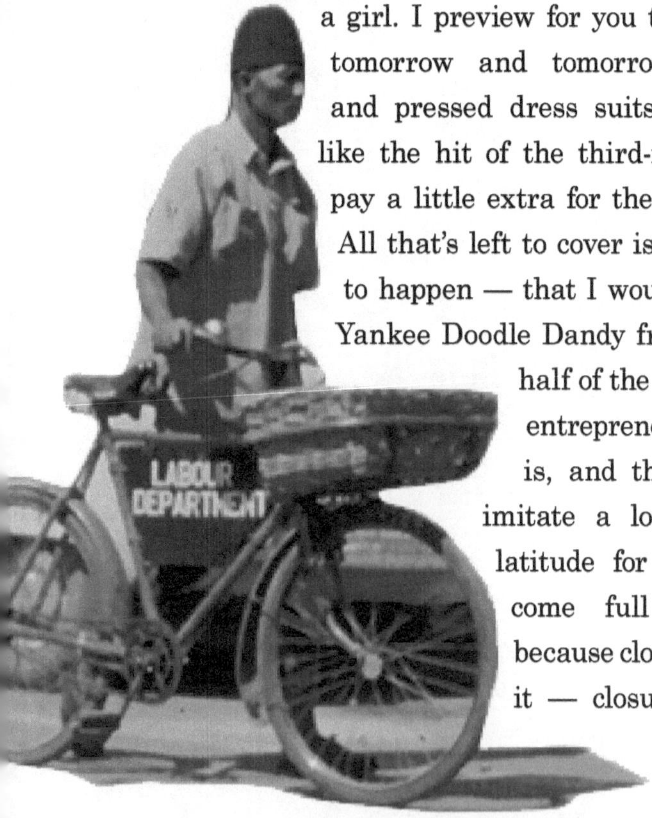

have a reputation to live down, that's all, and a theory of personality and ostensibly individual action, to wit, to appropriate Sartre for self:

> don't be led into believing that hotheadedness or an unhappy childhood gave him some odd liking for violence. He has made himself spokesman for the situation, nothing more.

The restorers retouched the painting. The harm is done being done; I couldn't step in that river again, even if I wanted to. But I don't. I want to go with the flow down the path of least resistance: turn off my mind and float downstream. I want to keep the message of the painting alive forever. Peace, dude, in a 21st-century package. And I want to keep myself in the style to which I've become accustomed. Or play the game "Existence" to the end. Of the beginning, of the beginning. You must remember that last one from the Beatles' *Revolver*. Name that Tune, Your Honor. Nope, it's "Tomorrow Never Knows." But today, please listen to the color of my dreams, and help me put an end to the double-dealing double agent of history who tried to spit in the

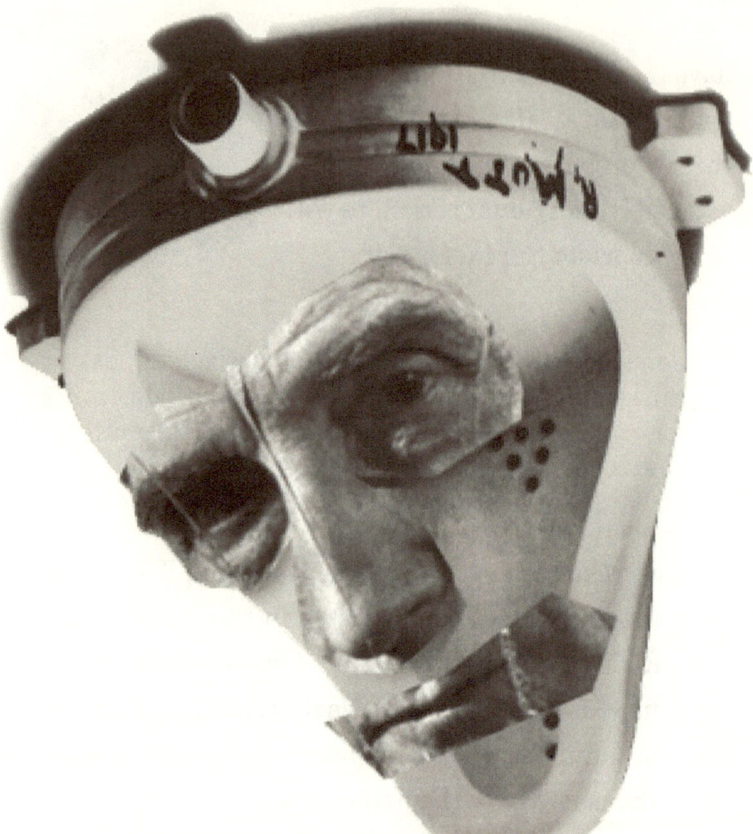

wind of it with spray paint on the likes of the world's greatest work of art. Let me go back to mine in the mines of the preservation of culture midtown. My mother thanks you. My father thanks you. My sister thanks you. And I thank you.

Brief

Textual References

Epigraph	Enright, D.J., "Vandalism." *London Review of Books*, XIII/17 (Sept. 12, 1991), 7.
18	"Jackson Visits Portrait and Says It's Inoffensive." *The New York Times* 4 Dec. 1989: C22.
19	Marcel Duchamp, as quoted in Alain Badiou, "Some Remarks Concerning Marcel Duchamp." Tilton Gallery, New York, NY. 16 Nov. 2007.
	Gamboni, Dario. *The Destruction of Art: Iconoclasm and Vandalism Since the French Revolution*. London: Reaktion, 1997. 295.
21	Rauschenberg, Robert, as quoted in Anna Moszynska, *Abstract Art*. London: Thames and Hudson, 1990. 197.
23, 26-27	Frost, Robert. "The Gift Outright." *The Poetry of Robert Frost*. Ed. Edward Connery Lathem. New York: Holt, Rinehart and Winston, 1969.
26, 31-35	Frost, Robert. "For John F. Kennedy, His Inauguration." *The Poetry of Robert Frost*. Ed. Edward Connery Lathem. New York: Holt, Rinehart and Winston, 1969.
29	"Atonal Antarctic." LXXVII No.1 *Time* (1961): n.pag.
36	"The Case of the Fickle Fortune." *Perry Mason*. Writ. Sol Stein and Glenn P. Wolfe. Dir. Laslo Benedek. CBS. 21 Jan. 1961.
	Heinlein, Robert. *Stranger in a Strange Land*. New York: Penguin, 1961. 206.
40	Booth, Wayne. *The Rhetoric of Fiction* Chicago: Toronto UP, 1961.

Textual References

45 Tomkins, Calvin. "Not Seen And/Or Less Seen." *The New Yorker* 6 Feb. 1965: 65.

45-46 Sullivan, Walter. "65% in Test Blindly Obey Order to Inflict Pain : Yale Experiment Shows Many Became Distraught Over Cruelty but Did Not Stop." *The New York Times* 26 Oct. 1963: 10.

48 Gould, Jack. "Exciting Television." *The New York Times* 5 Mar. 1961: X11.

49 Minow, Newton. "Television and Public Interest." National Association of Broadcasters, Washington, D.C. 9 May 1961.

49-50 Mitchell, Peter. "Brainwashed." *The New York Times* 5 May 1961: X16.

50 Reeves, Rosser. *Reality in Advertising.* New York: Knopf, 1961.

52 Checker, Chubby. "Pony Time." Rec. 1961. *The Best of Chubby Checker: Cameo Parkway* 1959-1963. Abkco, 2005.

53 "The Haven." *The Dupont Show with June Allyson.* CBS. 6 Mar. 1961.

53-55 Minow, ibid.

58 Sen. Byrd, Harry. "In Defense of Prince Edward County of Virginia." United States Senate, Washington, D.C. 17 May 1961.

60 United States. U.S Central Intelligence. *Family Jewels* Jan. 1975. <www.foia.cia.gov>.

63-64 Minow, ibid.

64-66 Bandura, Albert, Dorothea Ross, and Sheila Ross. "Transmission of Aggression Through Imitation of Aggressive Models." *The Journal of Abnormal and Social Psychology* 63 (1961): 575-582.

67-68	“France: To The Jugular.” LXXVII *Time* (1961): n.pag.
68-69	House, Jim, and Neil MacMaster. *Paris 1961: Algerians, State Terror, and Memory.* New York: Oxford University Press, 2006. 117-18.
69	Frost, Robert. “The Gift Outright.”
70-72	Goss, Steven. “A Partial Guide to the Tools of Art Vandalism.” *Cabinet* 1.3 (2001): n.pag. Web. <www.cabinetmagazine.org>.
72	“Article 3 – No Title.” *The New York Times* 13 Mar. 1914: 4.
73-74	“National Gallery Outrage. The Rokeby Venus. Suffragist Prisoner in Court. Extent of the Damage.” *Times* 11 Mar. 1914: 9.
74	Freedberg, David. *The Power of Images: Studies in the History and Theory of Response.* Chicago: University of Chicago Press, 1991. 502, footnote 72-73.
77	Bandura, Albert. Dorothea Ross, and Sheila Ross, ibid.
79	“Flavor & Extract Manufacturers’ Association: The First Seventy-Five Years.” 12-14. <www. FEMAFlavor.org>.
82	“Missile Bound Yogi.” *The Yogi Bear Show.* Writ. Warren Foster and Michael Maltese. Dir. Joseph Barbera and William Hanna. Warner Bros. 21 Oct. 1961.
83	Snodgrass, W.D. “Heart’s Needle.” *Heart’s Needle.* New York: Knopf, 1961.
88	“A Bear Living.” *The Yogi Bear Show.* Writ. Warren Foster and Michael Maltese. Dir. Joseph Barbera and William Hanna. Warner Bros. 8 May 1961.

Textual References

89-90	Loof, Susanna. "Lichtenstein Painting Vandalised." *Independent* 5 Sept. 2005: 19.
92	Hartley-Brewer, Julia. "Private Lives: Nothing to lose but our clothes Vincent Bethell is ready to go to jail for the right to bare all." *The Guardian* 15 Oct 1999: 6.
93	Josef Kleer, as quoted in Gamboni. 210.
	Louis Réau, as quoted in Dario Gamboni, *The Destruction of Art: Iconoclasm and Vandalism since the French Revolution.* London: Reaktion Books, 1997. 22.
99	United States. U.S Central Intelligence *Memorandum on Counterintelligence Activities.* Jul. 1962. <www.foia.cia.gov>.
106-07	Whispers, The. "This Time." Rec. 1983. *Love for Love.* Capitol, 1996.
107	Simon & Garfunkel. "Sounds of Silence." Rec. 1964. *Sounds of Silence.* Sony, 2001.
107	Checker, Chubby. "Let's Twist Again." Rec. 1961. *The Best of Chubby Checker: Cameo Parkway.* 1959-1963. Abkco, 2005.
108-09	Bandura, ibid.
110	Milgram, Stanley. *Obedience to Authority.* 1974. New York: Perennial Classics, 2004.
111-14	*Battle of Algiers.* Dir. Gillo Pontecorvo. Perfs. Brahim Hadjadj, Jean Martin, Saadi Yacef. 1966. DVD. Criterion Collection, 2004.
115-16	Braniff International Airways. "Braniff Airlines Commercial With Andy Warhol and Sonny Liston." 1968. Online Video Clip. Youtube.

119 Dohrn, Bernardine. "A Declaration of a State of War." *The Pacifica Radio/UC Berkeley Social Activism Sound Recording Project*. Web Transcript.

119-20 Zimbardo, Philip, et al. "The Mind is a Formidable Jailer: A Pirandellian Prison." *The New York Times Magazine* 8 Apr. 1973: 38.

120-21 Hofmann, Paul. "Pietà Damaged in Hammer Attack." Special to *The New York Times* 22 May 1972: 1.

126 Krebs, Albin. "Notes on People." *The New York Times* 23 Nov. 1977: 41.

128ff. Nochlin, Linda. "Why Have There Been No Great Women Artists?" *Women, Art, and Power and Other Essays*. New York: Harper & Row, 1988. 145-177.

133 Horacio Verbitsky, *The Silence*, extract transl. in English made available by *Open Democracy*: "Breaking the Silence: the Catholic Church in Argentina and the 'dirty war,'" July 28, 2005.

134 Joseph Pierre Proudhon, *Du principe de l'art et de sa destination sociale* (Paris, 1865) 63; as quoted in Dario Gamboni. 343, footnote 49.

135-37 "Girl Demolishes Louvre Painting; Slashes Ingres's 'Sistine Chapel' and Gives Herself Up to the Police." *The New York Times* 22 Sep. 1907: C4.

137-38 Freud, Sigmund. "Obsessive Acts and Religious Practices." *The Psychopathology of Everyday Life*. New York: Penguin Classics, 2003. 166.

138-39 Goss, ibid.

Textual References

141	Renzetti, Elizabeth. "Student Cannot Stomach Certain Famous Painting." *Globe and Mail.* 30 Nov. 1996: A1.
	DePalma, Anthony. "No Stomach for Art." *The New York Times* 8 Dec. 1996: E2.
142-44	Sartre, Jean-Paul. Preface. *The Wretched of the Earth.* 1961. By Frantz Fanon. New York: Grove, 2004.
146-48	Sartre, ibid.
145	Nochlin, ibid.
152	Paumgarten, Nick. "The $40-Million Elbow." *The New Yorker* 23 Oct. 2006: 32.
155-56	Kaufman, Michael. "'Guernica' Survives a Spray-Paint Attack by Vandal." *The New York Times* 1 Mar. 1974: 1-2.
156-58	Pilkington, Edward. "Life, Death and the Meaning of a Two-Tone Sheep Dip." *The Guardian* 19 Aug. 1994: 1.
158	Goss, ibid.
166	Justin Kaplan, *Walt Whitman: A Life.* New York: HarperCollins, 2003. 250.
168	72 Conn. 244, 43 A. 1047.
169	Elkins, James. *Why Are Our Pictures Puzzles? On The Modern Origins of Pictorial Complexity.* New York: Routledge, 1999. 16.
172	Kuntz, Katrina. "Why Art Vandals Strike." *f News* November 2005: n.pag. Web. <www.fnewsmagazine.com>.
177	Sartre, xlix.

Brief Visual References

The Adoration of the Golden Calf, Marc Chagall, 1966
Algerian massacre in Paris, collage
Andy Warhol
Astronaut

Baby on a Green Sofa, Lucian Freud, 1961
Baghdad City, bus map, 1961
Bamiyan Buddhas
Barney and Betty Hill's hands
Barney Rubble with TV
Barnyard Dawg
Baton Training, c. 1962, Orange County Sheriff Museum and Education Center
Bay of Naples, Cy Twombly, 1961
Bayer Dental Department brochure, designed by the Bayer-Team, *Graphis Annual* 65/66
Berlin Metro map, 1961
Beverly Station, B & M Railroad
Billy Williams, Chicago Cubs, Rookie of the Year, National League, 1961, his right hand
Billy Williams, Chicago Cubs, Rookie of the Year, National League, 1961, sliding into a base
The Birds, 1961
Black and white baby dolls
Bleu II, Joan Miró, 1961
Bozo the Clown with a child
Bozo the Clown in "The Mystery of the Missing Point," front page, 1961
The Brain That Wouldn't Die, still, 1962
Brion Gysin, *Word Flow*, 1961
Burgerville, Vancouver, 1961
Burning Conscience: The Case of the Hiroshima Pilot Claude Eatherly Told in His Letters to Gunther Anders, cover, 1961

Visual References

Butterfly
Butterick samples

Cindy Ray, tattoo artist, Australia, 1960
The Cleftones
"Closer Than We Think," Arthur Radebaugh, April 9, 1961
Coco Chanel, 1961
Constructing a ferrit core memory in the Zuse KG, 1961

Dedication, Robert Frost
Deltawerken, Haringvliet, Aart Klein, 1961
Deputy with rifle, c. 1958, Orange County Sheriff Museum & Education Center
DES molecule
Dexter King
Dick Clark
Diego Rivera at work
Disney dog
Disneyland clown

ECHO satellite, 1961
Elvis Presley
Eta'Della Pietra, cover, 1960

Fallout Shelter sign
Fannie Lou Hamer
Faster Pussycat, Kill, Kill
Fiat 1200 ad, 1961
The Fire Paintings, Yves Klein, 1961
Fountain, Marcel Duchamp, 1917
Frank O'Hara, Alice Neel, 1961

The Golden Pourer ad, 1961
Guernica, Pablo Picasso, 1937
Gulf Oil sign

H.M.S. Dreadnought
Hammer
Hilltop Steakhouse, Saugus, Massachusetts
House of Fiction, Artist unknown, c. 1960
Humphrey Bogart smoking

Indian Head Test Pattern
Inflatable punching clown
International Women's Day stamp, 1961

Jacinta Gil Poncalés, *Autoportrait*, 1961
James Brown, *Prisoner of Love*, 1961

Kevyn Burger and sister, 1961
Khertek Anchimaa-Toka, Deputy Chairperson of Oblast Executive Committee 1944-1961; Deputy Chairperson of the Council of Ministers of Tuva 1961-1972. Formerly Chairperson of the Women's Department of the Central Committee of the Tuvinian People's Revolutionary Party, and Head of State, People's Republic of Tannu Tuva

Laika, Soviet space dog, stamp, 1961
Leontyne Price as Liu in *Turandot*, hands, face, 1961
Literair Akkord, cover, 1960
Look magazine, January 31, 1961

Malcolm X's eyes and glasses
Map, Jasper Johns, 1961
Margaret Johnston in *Burn, Witch, Burn*, 1962
Martin Luther King, Jr.'s hands in handcuffs
Master Plan for the unbuilt New Town at Hook, Hampshire (Greater London Council, 1961)
The Misfits, 1961
My People, Lukta Qiatsuk Parr, 1961
Mothra, poster, 1961

Visual References

Nam June Paik, *Video Still*
Nine Tomorrows, Isaac Asimov, 1959, cover
No. 13, Mark Rothko

1, Octavian font, designed in 1961

Packers-Bears Game, September 23, 1960
Panorama City Hospital, Opening Day, 1962
Person passing by the Arusha Safari Hotel, Tanzania, 1961
Person vomiting
Pharmaceutical Prospectus, Hans Schweiss, *Gebrauchsgraphik* No. 10, 1961
Pig Eyes – Part 1, Nat Kendrick, 1961
The Pietà, Michelangelo
Portrait of the Artist's Mother, Rembrandt, c. 1629
Prehistoric hand
Proposed Railways, China, 1961

Raggedy Ann
Railroad tracks
Red Painting, Cy Twombly, 1961
Relation between the 50% retention length and the value of catch size times selection factor (Bohl and Koura, 1962) in "Biological Data on the Common Shrimp, *crangon crangon* (Linnaeus, 1758)" in *Proceedings of the World Scientific Conference on the Biology and Culture of Shrimps and Prawns*, 1967
Revolver, The Beatles, cover, 1966
Rice College hijinks, 1960
Richard Milhous Nixon likeness
Rotary International, 52nd Annual Convention, "Impressions from Japan," Tokyo, 1961
Rotary telephone, 1961
Royal Doulton figurine, Girl in Pink Dress Curtsying

Saigon, 1962
Sinclair dinosaur
Six Mile Bottom, Frank Stella, 1970
Smokey the Bear Fire Prevention PSA, c. 1967
Soviet tools
St. John's Anglican Church in Westphal
Story, Philip Guston, 1978
The Story of a Novel: the genesis of Doctor Faustus, Thomas Mann, cover, 1961
Stranger in a Strange Land, cover, 1961 edition

Target, Jasper Johns, 1958
Telstar satellite, 1961
Texaco Station, 1960
Three Women, Park Soo-keun, 1961
To Martha's Memory, Jiro Yoshihara, 1961
Tomato
Training Academy patrol briefing, c. 1962, Orange County Sheriff Museum & Education Center
Treble and bass clef signs from John Cage score
Tropic of Cancer, Henry Miller, Grove Press edition, 1961
TV Guide, page A58, February 17, 1961
TV static

U.N. ad for Comfort Women
U.S. Department of Commerce, National Weather Service, North Atlantic Hurricane Tracking Chart, 1961
Untitled, Clyfford Still, 1961
Untitled, Helen Frankenthaler, 1961
Untitled Anthropometry, Yves Klein, 1960

Vanya Élias-Jose, São Paolo Library Hall performance, 1961
Venus de Milo
Vir Heroicus Sublimis, Barnett Newman, 1950-51

Visual References

We Two Boys Together Clinging, David Hockney, 1961
White kids on a stoop
White woman with missile
Wohnmobile Motor Home, Mercedes Benz 0321H, 1961
A Woman in the Sun, Edward Hopper, 1961
Wonderful World of Disney
The Wretched of the Earth, cover, 1961 edition

Zwan *soepballetjes* ad
Zygote

Acknowledgements

Thanks to Ella Boureau and Hazel Lee Santino for their imaginative work with images.

Thanks to Scott Peterman for writing kick-ass code, for entering into the mind of the work, and for expert guidance into the 21st Century.

Thanks to Debra Di Blasi for her intelligence, her creativity, her range, and her persistence of vision.

Thanks without end to David Jauss for his mighty fine mind, for his outrageous generosity with his time and his black ink, for all his encouragement, and for his unexcelled example as a reader, writer, editor, mentor, and human being.

Thanks to Cathy Crane for everything. Thanks to Zoa Chasin and Gray Sansom-Chasin for their every-daily radiance, hilarity, and heart, for snuggles, for growing me, and for joy upon joy.

I acknowledge – and marvel at – Chaos and Serendipity, who roll....

About the Author

Alexandra Chasin received a PhD in Modern Thought and Literature at Stanford University in 1993, and an MFA in Fiction Writing at Vermont College in 2002. Chasin is the author of *Selling Out: The Gay and Lesbian Movement Goes to Market*, a study of the relation between the LGBT "market" and the LGBT social movement, and of *Kissed By*, a collection of short formally innovative fiction. Past recipient of a Bunting Fellowship at Radcliffe, a Whiting Dissertation Fellowship, and a 2012 Fiction Fellowship from New York Foundation for the Arts, Chasin teaches in the Literary Studies Department at Eugene Lang College, The New School for Liberal Arts.

www.ingramcontent.com/pod-product-compliance
Lightning Source LLC
Chambersburg PA
CBHW030831020726
47499CB00006B/2159
* 9 7 8 1 9 3 7 5 4 3 2 4 2 *